THE ANNIVERSARY OF NEVER

The Anniversary of Never

by

Joel Lane

Swan River Press
Dublin, Ireland
MMXXI

The Anniversary of Never
by Joel Lane

Published by
Swan River Press
Dublin, Ireland
in September, MMXXI

www.swanriverpress.ie
brian@swanriverpress.ie

Introduction © Nicholas Royle
All stories © Estate of Joel Lane
except "Ashes in the Water"
© Estate of Joel Lane & Mat Joiner
This edition © Swan River Press

Cover design by Meggan Kehrli
from "Fleeting" © Polly Rose Morris

Set in Garamond by Ken Mackenzie

Paperback Edition
ISBN 978-1-78380-749-9

Swan River Press published
a limited hardback edition of
The Anniversary of Never in August 2015.

Contents

Introduction

I walk up Holland Park Avenue to Tony Benn's house. The front door is open and I wander in. The first thing I see is a dog, and a man I don't recognise. It's not Tony Benn, that's for sure. I become aware of a group of people sitting in a circle. Soon I realise I have stumbled upon a recording of TV panel show *QI*. I recognise Joel Lane and Andy Brown. I leave, with Andy, and go to a nearby café where there are beautifully designed cruet sets, with very tall and slender pieces that sit in a kind of cradle. They can't be very useful, but they are attractive.

I had this dream on 28 August 2010. I don't watch *QI*, so I don't know why I should have dreamt about it. I did once meet Tony Benn, as he got out of a taxi outside his house, which was indeed located on the north side of Holland Park Avenue in west London. I said hello to him and he put his bag down on the pavement and chatted to me for a good five minutes. Andy Brown was an external examiner working for Manchester Metropolitan University, where I lecture in creative writing. Andy's regular employer was the University of Exeter, and Exeter was the birthplace of my great friend Joel Lane, which is how I think Andy came to appear in the dream. Why *QI*, though? I can only think it was because Joel was extremely intelligent. Joel would also have been, like me, an admirer of Tony Benn. In fact, I have a vague memory of telling him about meeting Benn and him responding with an anecdote about bumping into Michael Foot, perhaps on a protest march or anti-war rally. Or it's equally possible I'm dreaming that as well.

My first recorded dream involving Joel, dating from 18 March 1996, saw him, or, more accurately, someone who looked like him, playing in a football match. The player who looks like Joel gets injured and while he is receiving treatment, I pan around, like a cameraman, and see that his nostril has been badly torn like Jack Nicholson's in *Chinatown*. Before the resulting free kick can be taken, a lorry drives on to the pitch, blocking most of the goal.

The only other dream I can find in my notebooks in which Joel appears is dated 17 February 2003 and reads simply: "I was taking a bath with Joel."

Taking? Since when do I *take* a bath? I *have* baths.

After my dad died, in September 1994 (less than a week before I published Joel's debut short story collection), I would see him coming towards me in the street. I would find myself standing behind him in a supermarket queue. He would be sitting at the wheel of a car waiting for a red light to change. A bereavement counsellor assured me the phenomenon was common and quite normal.

In his story "The North London Book of the Dead", Will Self writes about a man whose mother dies. The narrator describes "an intense period during which I kept seeing people in the street who I thought were Mother". He goes on: "I'd be walking in the West End or the City and there, usually on the other side of the road, would be Mother, ambling along staring in shop windows." When he gets closer "the likeness would evaporate. Not only wasn't it Mother, but it seemed absurd that I ever could have made the mistake. The late-middle-aged woman looked nothing like Mother . . . " Each time it happens, "the fact that Mother was dead hit me again, it was as if it hadn't really occurred to me before and that her failure to get in touch with me over the past six months had been solely because she was 'hellishly busy' ".

This gets close to reflecting some of the bafflement and perplexity I felt after Joel died. My dad had been terminally ill; we knew the end was coming. Joel had chronic conditions but they were not thought to be life-threatening. When he went to bed on Monday, 25 November 2013, a few weeks after celebrating his fiftieth birthday, he would have had no idea he would not be waking up in the morning.

Life goes on, but the world has changed. I couldn't make sense of the fact that Joel wasn't around any more. I wouldn't hear his quiet, breathy voice on the phone again ("Hi, how're things with you?"). I wouldn't read any more of his extraordinarily generous critiques of my stories (reading far more into them than I'd ever intended). I would never again walk alongside him past groups of vaguely threatening young men outside various Black Country railway stations.

Time passes and you don't so much forget as stop being constantly aware of someone's absence, and then something happens—you're searching for a book on your shelves and you spot the copy of Thomas Tryon's *The Other* he gave you or you've got your iPod on shuffle and up pops a track by the Nightingales that you only know because he gave you one of their albums—and, like Self's bereaved narrator, you are brutally reminded.

Joel Lane was an enormously gifted novelist, short story writer, anthologist and poet. He was born in 1963 and lived most of his life in Birmingham. He was a great friend to many—professionals and non-professionals alike—in the field of what he liked to call weird fiction. His short stories were collected, during his too-brief lifetime, in *The Earth Wire & Other Stories* (1994), *The Lost District & Other Stories* (2006), *The Terrible Changes* (2009), *Do Not Pass Go* (2011) and *Where Furnaces Burn* (2012).

When Brian J. Showers, the publisher of Swan River Press, invited me to write this introduction, I asked him if the collection had a theme. He shared with me a line from an email he had received from Joel, for, while the collection may be a posthumous publication, it was not planned that way: "*The Anniversary of Never* is a group of stories concerned with the theme of the afterlife and the idea that we may enter the afterlife before death, or find parts of it in our world."

I have been an admirer of Joel's work since I read his story, "The Foggy, Foggy Dew", when it was reprinted in Karl Edward Wagner's *The Year's Best Horror Stories XV* in 1986. Over the years he wrote some of the creepiest and most frightening stories ("Face Down", "The Window") and some of the most powerfully moving stories I have ever read ("The Only Game", "Without a Mind"), but that idea, "that we may enter the afterlife before death, or find parts of it in our world", is sublime. It reminds me of what Joel wrote in my copy of *The Terrible Changes*: "Another few postcards from the earthly paradise."

I have always been drawn to visions of the afterlife, in fiction and film, glimpses of heaven in particular. Even while I have no faith, I do want to believe. I can't bear the thought of the void. The narrator of "The Only Game" recalls his partner's reassurances: "Other people are part of us. Missing them shows that we're still connected to them, we still need them. It's the love we need to hold on to. The life, not the death."

It's tempting to think of dreams as offering a form of afterlife, if only for the living. I have dreamt of my dad many times since he died and in almost all of those dreams, for the duration of the dream, I felt that he was alive. The dreams made me happy, and there was no dismayed realisation upon waking, no feeling that I had been deceived by the dream. One dream was different; in it my dad was watching my son and a friend of my son's at play, but my dad looked grey and lifeless. *This is supposed to give you energy*, I said to him, but I knew it was hopeless. He really was dead and I felt a great sadness.

If I have dreamt of Joel since he died, I have not remembered those dreams upon waking, but that may be partly due to the fact that I'm remembering fewer dreams, perhaps as I get older. Nevertheless, I'm optimistic Joel will turn up sooner or later. I even draw some comfort from the thought that he may have already done so and I've simply failed to remember and record the dream.

We are fortunate to have a new collection of Joel's stories, especially in what I am sure will be a beautiful edition with an exquisite cover illustration by Polly Rose Morris. Several of these stories represent Joel, a brilliant short story writer, at his very best. "Other people are part of us . . . It's the love we need to hold on to. The life, not the death."

Nicholas Royle
May 2015

The Anniversary of Never

Sight Unseen

In October 2008, I had a call from my mother to let me know my father had died. I offered to go and see her, but she said it wasn't necessary. We live about thirty miles apart. Apparently I was down as his next of kin. Which surprised me, as I hadn't been sure he was still alive. Neither of us had seen him since 1982.

"There are some things of his you're entitled to," my mother said. "Not much. He was living in a hostel. His body was found in Salford."

"What happened to him?" I asked.

"They don't seem to know. Maybe a stroke or a heart attack. Someone found him near the river, just lying there. That's care in the community, I suppose." Her voice sounded brittle.

"Are you sure you're okay?"

"It's just a shock, David." She paused. "If you'd told me a week ago he was still alive, I'd have said I didn't give a fuck. He left us both. But now I can't help wondering what happened to him. The police said he was living there alone, no partner, nothing. Maybe they came for him after all."

"Who?" She didn't answer. "Oh, you mean . . . But if so they didn't take him, did they?"

"Maybe they didn't like what they found. Oh don't worry, David. I'm not going mad. I'm just upset. And I'm sad for you. All these years."

"Don't worry. I'm all right." The part of me that cared was lost in time. It might as well have been abducted by aliens.

"The police want to talk to you." She gave me a number with an 0161 prefix: Manchester. "There'll be an inquest. Oh, something I forgot—he was registered blind. Don't know why he went out somewhere on his own."

"People's habits don't change."

She laughed quietly. "I'll speak to you soon, David. Take care."

"And you." I put the phone down and stared at the number I'd written on a scrap of paper. In the window, the September daylight was fading. The grey wall of next door's garage was marked with some regular scratches that didn't quite make an image. I reached for the keypad, then realised my fingers were trembling too much to dial.

I don't remember my father very clearly. He left home when I was seven. After that, my mother destroyed every picture of him that had been in the house. I remember him as a thin man with dark hair, angular cheekbones, and uneven teeth. But that may all be inaccurate.

What I'm sure of is that when the sun went down, he would never put the light on unless he wanted to read. I remember him and my mother arguing about it. "It's not safe," she'd say. "David could walk into something and hurt himself." He would say that artificial light cost money.

Another thing I recall is his collection of fossils. They were in the front room, on the shelves of the bookcase. Some were entire shells turned to stone; others were polished surfaces that held skeletons, whorls, segmented forms. He let me hold them, said it was like being able to touch the past. Behind the fossils, the shelves were full of his books about UFOs and pyramids and magic. He said I could read them when I was old enough. But by then he'd gone and taken the books with him, and I wouldn't have wanted to read them anyway.

It's hard for me to separate what I saw then from what my mother told me later. My father started coming and going at odd hours, sometimes just sitting in the front room when the rest of us got up in the morning. Sometimes he wouldn't speak to me or my mother all day. Then they'd start arguing during the night. *My body's not my own*, he said. *This life is a disguise. They'll come for me again. I don't belong here.* It didn't make any sense to me—or to my mother, who shouted that he needed to get help, he was going mad, he was a danger to me.

In retrospect, of course, he was going through a breakdown. And my mother did succeed in getting him onto medication, though he said she was just trying to stop him seeing. I'm not sure exactly what he believed, but the core of it was that he had been abducted by aliens when he was a teenager. They wanted to use him as an observer, he said. He told me several times that if I was approached by anyone who wasn't human, too pale or thin to be a person, I should tell him at once.

Shortly before he left, he started going into trance-like states. He'd stop whatever he was doing, then move his head slowly like a camera. "They want to see," he explained when my mother tried to make him snap out of it. A few times she broke down, wept with frustration and grief at what was happening to him. He cried too, wrapping his face in his hands, shaking. There was a terrible darkness in his eyes. I started to believe he really wasn't human.

One night I heard my mother screaming and jerked awake in the dark, trying to hear and not hear at the same time. *What do they want to see? This? What do you want me* to show them? *You're mad. Get out of here. Get out! GET OUT!* I heard him walk slowly down the stairs. My mother carried on crying. I curled up in the bed, my hands over my ears, a noose of tension gripping my throat.

The next day, my father packed a suitcase and left. He came back for the rest of his possessions during the week, while I was at school. The house felt invaded by emptiness. My mother said it was better for him not to be there at all than to be there in body but somewhere else in his mind. I didn't show her the note he'd left on my bed. *Dear David,* it said, *I'm sorry to leave you, but this isn't what I am. I need to find my real self. One day you'll see and understand. Love always, Dad.* I stole a few matches from the kitchen, then took the note to the local wasteground and burned it.

My father didn't try to keep in touch after the divorce went through. We knew he'd moved to Wales. When people asked, my mother said he was on another planet. I was vaguely aware of missing him, but the thought was bound up with resentment and fear. *Fuck it,* I thought eventually. *If he doesn't want to know me, I don't want to know him.* There was no surrogate father either, though after I left home there were men in my life. But never for too long. I always walked away before they had the chance to abandon me.

The train from Birmingham to Manchester passed through the badlands of the north Midlands, stopping at Derby and Stoke-on-Trent as if to make a point. The view was crowded with damaged factories, rusting sheets of corrugated iron, grey brick walls tattooed with bright swirls of spray paint. A station waiting room with tatters of broken glass like loose skin in its windows. How could people live in ruins?

I was vaguely aware of the sounds in the train carriage. A child imitating mechanical noises, a young woman on the phone to her lover, a dog barking out of sight. But I felt like a camera focused on the images beyond the window. Had my father's blindness been caused by some hereditary disease? Did I have that to look forward to? Beyond that, more difficult questions were lurking. What would it have been like if he'd stayed with us? Would I understand him? Questions that couldn't be asked, let alone answered.

At Manchester Piccadilly I was met by Steve Cohn, a plain-clothes police officer I'd spoken to on the phone. Where non-suspects are concerned the police are a lot less formal than they used to be. We picked up coffees at the station, and he drove me to a nearby park overlooked by flaking tower blocks. "I'm sorry about your dad," he said.

The coffee tasted like tarnished metal. "It was a long time ago," I said. "There's nothing to go back to. He changed."

"I need a statement from you. Nothing too detailed. And then I'll be happy to answer any questions you have. If I know the answers."

The statement established that I'd had no contact with my father for twenty-five years, and that I had no claim on his estate (such as it was) beyond the standard legal rights. I also volunteered the information that I'd suspected he was mentally ill, but hadn't tried to contact him for family reasons. My words didn't taste much better than the coffee, but the policeman didn't offer any comment.

When he'd recorded my statement, I asked: "Could I see his room?"

"I'm afraid it's been cleared out. But his possessions are at the coroner's offices in Salford. I can arrange for you to see them and take anything you'd like to keep, as long as you have ID on you." I did. "One hostel room is very much like another," Cohn said. "To be honest, all it will tell you is that he lived in a very limited space."

"That's not how I think of him. At least he died in the open air. Could I see where . . . "

"Of course." Cohn gave me a photocopied page from a map, with an X marked in red next to the river Irwell. "There's a slope they call the Landslide, where a street collapsed in 1927. Your dad was lying at the bottom of the slope, looking up into the sky. He wasn't entirely blind, you know. He could see a bright light."

"What was wrong with his eyes?"

"Some kind of tumour. He'd had a few operations for it, so the tissue around his eyes was badly scarred. He'd been on and off radiotherapy for years. That could have brought on the seizure that killed him. The people who found your dad, some local teenagers, said he was reaching up in the air."

I didn't ask if I could see him. Often I wish I had. I'd been struggling with that all day, finally decided to ask, but when it came down to it I was afraid. That the old man's face wouldn't inspire any recognition in me. That his damaged eyes would see through me. I bit my lip.

Cohn drove me to Salford. It reminded me of north Birmingham: new roads, garages, and fast-food restaurants juxtaposed with much older, all but derelict housing. He stopped outside the coroner's office. "I'll come in with you." He spoke to the receptionist, who checked my Council Tax booklet and called someone on the phone. "I'll leave you to get on with it," Cohn said. "Feel free to contact me if you have any questions. Take care."

A tall, bald man appeared, blinked at me as if I were a neon sign, then led me down a corridor and through several fire doors to an office at the back of the building. He unlocked the door and said, "Alan Kinver's things are in this room on the left. Take your time, and put aside anything you'd like to keep. You'll need to fill in some forms, but that won't take long. I'll come back in an hour to see how you're getting on."

The office was lined with metal shelves bearing grey plastic crates, like a warehouse. Nine crates had stickers marked with my father's name and date of death. I moved them all to the floor, then sat on a chair to examine their contents. The first two were shirts, trousers and shoes—faded, torn, and dusty, nothing a charity shop would have accepted. The third was cooking pans and crockery that hadn't been cleaned in a long time. The fourth was an assortment: two white plastic sticks, a traditional walking-stick, a compass, a pair of binoculars, a small telescope, a radio, and a wristwatch with a cracked face, the hands stuck at three o'clock.

At the bottom of the fourth crate was a flat cardboard box that opened at the top. It was full of small chunks or flakes of stone, each bearing a fossil. There were coiled ammonites, segmented trilobites, white *dastilbe* or fossil fish, a leaf, a bird's skull, some kind of crayfish. He'd probably bought most of them in craft shops or museums, though a few rougher ones might have come from beaches. I closed the box and put it by my chair to take home.

The next two crates were full of books. All of the kind I remembered from the house in Smethwick: encounters with aliens, UFOs, the occult, theosophy, the Kabbalah, pyramids, ley lines. Most were dog-eared paperbacks from the sixties and seventies, but a few were older and more scarce hardbacks from specialist publishers. I took half a dozen of the latter to give me some insight into my father's world. By this time, my eyes were blurred with tears.

The seventh crate contained old sheets and blankets. They didn't rise up and make faces at me, but they were badly stained and had a faintly acrid, metallic smell I had to assume was my father's. The eighth crate contained several dozen cassettes—electronic, jazz, and modern classi-cal music—and a portable cassette player, plus a hundred or so yellowing issues of *Prediction*, *Fortean Times*, and similar magazines. Again there were some rarer titles, but I left them alone.

The bald man dropped by to check how I was. I told him I was okay and would go back to reception when I'd finished. The ninth crate was filled with paperwork. Note-books of various shapes and sizes, loose-leaf binders and folders, letters in opened envelopes, press cuttings about disappearances and mysterious sightings. I opened a small memo book and read:

> I am a witness, a living satellite. My eyes are alien. What my eyes record goes to their world, but the white people don't tell me what it means to them. My mind is human, but my eyes are not. The doctors deny that because they know. If they were merely ignorant, the facts would destroy them. Their role is to see nothing. Mine is to see every-thing. What a privilege, and what a terrible price.

My father's handwriting was small and blocky, like the text on an old home computer. It was hard to read—not be-cause it was untidy, but because the letters had been sim-plified to vestiges intended for his eyes only. A diary for 2005 was densely inscribed with notes and symbols that seemed to combine physics, astrology, and ritual magic. Certain dates were highlighted in red and given old-fash-ioned names: *Roodmass*, *May Eve*, *Hallowmass*. Time after time, with the imperishable faith of a Jehovah's Witness, he'd written: *They will come for me.*

One hard-bound notebook seemed more recent: the larger, more chaotic handwriting suggested a time when my father's sight was failing. On a typical page, the words were slanting up and down and any attempt at structure had been abandoned. The notes were half prayer and half solitary rant:

> a cold flame in the night—a promise never kept—the phases of a different moon—the coiled staircase inside—the language of fossils—these eyes aren't mine—a secret path through the rock—a woman with stars in her breasts—the smell of rotting stone—the eternal witness—trapped between worlds—never able to belong

Somewhere near the bottom of the last crate, I found a few small manila envelopes that contained photographs. One I remembered as having been on the wall above one of my father's bookcases: a blind white salamander that lived in underground rivers. Its eyelids were sealed, and it had pale feathery feelers on either side of its head. Suddenly I heard my father saying: *This is an olm.*

Another envelope contained two small photos in black and white. The first was of a small child I didn't recognise, walking on a wall; his face was in sunlight, laughing. Could that be a stepbrother I'd never met? Then I looked at the second photo and recognised my mother as a young woman. The child was me. I stared at the image, trying to see another face through it.

The cobbled street ended in a jagged ledge. The slope from there down to the Irwell was too steep to walk down steadily. Loose bricks and cobblestones lay between tree roots and jutted from mounds of earth. The surface was overgrown with moss and grasses, but showed little evidence of post-disaster human activity. It was like the war damage that survived in parts of Manchester and East London: if you couldn't repair it, you got used to it.

I worked my way cautiously down the slope, holding onto pieces of rubble to keep my balance. How had my father managed it? And more to the point, why? It had to be one of the places and times he'd marked out for *contact*. Because it was exposed and largely abandoned, or for some deeper reason to do with the psychic residue of the landslide? I couldn't fathom his thinking any more now than in the past. Words from his insane diary rattling through my head, I climbed over the shapeless ruins to the wooden bridge in the crevice of the valley. That was where they'd found him.

It was beginning to get dark, at least this far below street level. There were no streetlights down here, and it would be dangerous to stay much longer. But I couldn't help pausing on the bridge, crouching, letting my gaze climb slowly from the trees on the far bank to the slate-grey university buildings, and on into the dull evening sky. Threads of light were tangled among masses of torn cloud. I felt a buried excitement—part fear and part anticipation—grip me as I waited there. But only nightfall happened. I tried to say goodbye to my father, but the words wouldn't come. All I could think of was his still body lying here on the bridge, his damaged eyes gazing into the sky as if back up a flight of stairs he'd fallen down.

Several hours later, I was drinking in a basement bar near Whitworth Street. I'd booked a cheap hotel room in case the police and coroner business took longer than expected, but that was all in hand. The books, papers, and other bits and pieces I'd salvaged from my father's possessions were back at the hotel. Now I just needed something to escape into. Alcohol, music, and decent-looking men would serve that purpose. They generally did.

The bar was done out in a mock-warehouse style: cheaply whitewashed stone walls decorated with Tom of Finland prints, empty oil drums for seats. The music was a subdued pulse of techno. The air was cool, and the beer was cold. Middle-aged guys in leather vests and trousers mingled with younger, more brightly-dressed lads from the dance floor who'd come down here to chill out. I got talking to one of the latter, a dark-haired youth with bruised eyes and a flat Salford accent. We went upstairs and danced together for a while. Nothing more. That was as much contact as I needed.

A few nights later, I had a dream that woke me up breathless and shivering. I was sitting at my desk, reading, while night fell outside. Then I got up to close the curtains. In the window, I could see a classic harvest moon: yellow and almost full, its scars clearly visible. It was moving steadily downward and to the left. In another minute, it had dropped out of the sky. The scientific part of my mind informed me that, according to Newton's laws of motion, such a dramatic change in the moon's orbit around the earth would displace the earth from its own orbit around the sun. I gazed into a suddenly empty night sky, realising that all human life was going to end within a few hours.

On the last evening in October, I caught a bus out to the Sandwell Valley: a region of woodland with patches of open ground and a few wartime bomb shelters. It was a couple of miles from the house I'd lived in as a child, and I knew it had been one of my father's favourite places. These days I had friends who went there to cruise, but open-air sex had never been my thing. In fact, I couldn't really have explained why I was going there.

On the way, I saw a bunch of teenagers mooching from house to house in plastic ghost masks. Early fireworks cracked open the sky above the terraced houses. I was thinking of my father's last, barely readable diary: *you can't go through—you're caught between worlds—trapped in time like a fossil in stone.* Over the past few weeks, I'd been alternating between grief, bitterness, and indifference towards him. Gradually I'd become aware that these feelings were held in different layers of my own past. I wondered if he'd struggled with that too.

By the light of a half-moon and some constellations I didn't recognise, I made my way down into the forest. Dead leaves and branches obliterated the footpath. The smell of decay mingled with fresh smoke. I could hear the trickling of a river, but didn't see it. The sense of buried excitement returned to me, making me so tense it was an effort to breathe. I remembered my adolescent dreams of gypsies, hunters, outlaws. The eyes watching from the darkness. The moon clouded over until I had to reach in front of me to fend off overhanging branches. Then the foliage thinned out, and I felt a cold wind blowing through an open space ahead.

Without the trees, I could see the blurred orange glow of the city's light pollution. And something flickering and shifting on the edge of vision, like a distant fire but not bright enough, unless it was wrapped in smoke. The ground under my feet was harder than before. As my eyes adjusted to the near-dark, I saw that I was approaching a hilltop on which some kind of stone circle had been left to fall apart. Was this an observation point from wartime? The ruins looked much older than that. Then I glimpsed a thin figure waiting among the stones.

He stepped forward to meet me. I couldn't breathe. What could I say to him? *How have you been, apart from dying?* As he came closer, I saw he was moving his head slowly from side to side. Was that a message? Then the moonlight grew brighter, and I saw his face. The next thing I remember is running, tripping over roots, stumbling through branches, tearing my hands, not caring how much I hurt myself if the pain could help me believe that I hadn't seen white feelers reaching out of his eyes.

Eventually I realised I was back in the streets, somewhere on the edge of north Birmingham. The houses looked unreal, like a film set hastily constructed and damaged to give the impression of age. A black cab drove past and I waved it down. The driver was concerned, wanted to take me to the City Hospital, but I asked him to take me home. He gave me some tissues to clean the blood from my hands before I sat down. "Been in a fight?" he asked. I shook my head.

When I got back to my flat, it was just after midnight. I locked and bolted the door, checked the window locks, then went into the bedroom and pulled down the blind. But I didn't undress, or turn out the light. I got my electric torch from the bathroom in case the light-bulb failed. Then I sat on the bed, reading film magazines and waiting for the dawn. At some point, a memory came back to me that had been lost for years: how for a long time after my father left, I used to sleep with the bedside lamp on for fear of what I might learn to see in the dark.

Crow's Nest

Christmas was a bastard. It meant staying with his parents, sleeping in the tiny room he'd slept in as a kid. Which made Kevin feel like an old man at twenty-three, and reminded him that he had no-one else to spend Christmas with. And the damp in the house didn't help. The shadows in the walls became more grotesque each year. It was subsidence, his father said, affecting the whole area. North Birmingham was slowly drowning.

For some reason, this year he was finding it harder than usual not to think about his mother and the reasons why she'd left. Kevin always got a Christmas card from her, but he hadn't seen her in twelve years. She'd left the country and he'd not even left the district. He didn't mind Sue, his father's girlfriend—but the two of them had their own version of normality that didn't make sense to him, because of how it had been in the past.

Going to the bathroom in the early hours of the morning, he'd glimpsed two figures twisted together in the hallway. Their bodies were nearly transparent, like smoked glass. The man was pulling the woman's head back by her hair, and she was raising a knee towards his gut. He walked carefully around them before closing the bathroom door behind him. The cold air gripped his bowels.

Boxing Day was an afternoon in the pub, then a three-mile walk to the tower block that at least kept him out of reach of the water table. Kevin had six days before he went back to work. Six nights of booze, maybe some live music, maybe a chance to find a girl. There was always talent around at Christmas. And those dark nights just before the New Year were as bare and needy as a shaved pubis.

But this year, the cold trapped him in his flat. The frost on the windows like sheets of old newsprint, the blank sky that let every trace of warmth escape. The ammonia reek of the staircase seemed worse than ever, probably because there was more piss for it to cover up. When he did get out, the fear kept pace with him. He wished there was a little snow to soften the pavements, make the black trees glitter, absorb the echoes of the past. Any white powder would do.

Walking around Kingstanding in the daytime, he was shocked at how old the buildings seemed. It had always been a patchwork: new expressways and all-hours stores grafted onto housing estates and far older terraces. But nothing looked fresh any more. The concrete was stained with damp, the houses blurred and out of true. It was like a black and white film, or someone else's memory.

Where the hell had his friends gone? The pubs were half empty apart from sad old men and pikey teenagers dressed like rockers. And the NF boys where they always were, round the tables at the back of the White Lion, going nowhere. He'd hung out with them in his teens, lost interest when he realised how utterly lonely they were. And when he'd got involved with Theresa. Where had she got to?

Then he saw little Marky in the toilets at the Royal George. He was just standing by the wall, staring into space. Kevin wondered if what they'd said about him at school had been true. Or maybe he was on something. Kevin nodded and said "Hi", but Marky didn't react. When Kevin turned around from the urinal, there was nobody there: just a dark stain on the wall. Maybe that was all he'd seen, after six bottles of Diamond White.

He left the pub then, afraid of what else he might see if he didn't sober up. The cold air slapped him in the face. His breath trailed from his mouth like pale vomit. In the car park, two lads were kicking the shit out of someone. Kevin didn't see who, didn't care. Lots of people had it coming. As he walked away somewhat unsteadily, it occurred to him that he'd seen Marky get a few beatings in their schooldays. He might even have joined in. Maybe that was why the nonce had ignored him.

Near the King's Road estate, his mouth suddenly filled with bile. Kevin turned off the road so no-one would see him throw up. Beyond a cluster of black trees, he came to the edge of a long downward slope he remembered from his childhood. The moonlight glinted from frozen lakes, frost-covered roofs, car parks, the smoke of factory chimneys. His nausea slowly faded. From here, he could see past Spaghetti Junction and the Aston Expressway to the hard lights of the city centre.

Kevin thought of something he'd said to Theresa, years ago when they were a couple: he'd like to scatter the pieces of home over the slope, then go down there and put them back together. He wasn't even sure what he'd meant by that. The view from Kingstanding, a crow's nest high above the city, had excited him in those days. Now it made him feel exposed. But he stood there for a while, feeling the moonlight on his face, until the cold ground made his feet ache.

The last night before New Year's Eve, he went to see a band in Walsall—which was much nearer Kingstanding than the centre of Birmingham was. The band was some local indie-rock outfit called Triangle. They'd put out an album in the early nineties, hadn't done much since. The singer was a thin, rather manic Black Country Irish bloke with red eyes and a harsh guitar style. The songs were mostly about brutal sex, alcohol, and madness. The band played as if they were just on the edge of losing control.

Afterwards, feeling a bit shaken, Kevin caught the last bus to Great Barr and walked home from there. Jagged guitar riffs echoed in his mind. Suddenly he felt sure he'd read that Triangle's singer had died years ago. From a head injury. Was that just a rumour? Or had they found a new vocalist? Most of the old bands that were still going had new people, were pretty much their own tribute bands. At least Triangle played like they still meant it.

You didn't see that kind of rage any more. Musicians were so up themselves, the slightest twinge of pain and they were running to the therapist and selling their childhood traumas to the paper. No-one was allowed to say that life was shit. You had to register for a victim card and then play it every time. Well, fuck that. They could roll up their *support network* and put it where the sun didn't shine. Social workers and therapists were fit for happy slapping.

On New Year's Eve, Kevin paid ten quid to get into the King and Country. It was packed out, and by normal closing time everyone was wrecked. He could have pulled quite easily, but the music put him off. It was impossible to be seductive with Roy Wood or Slade as your soundtrack. The only Christmas song he didn't hate was the Pogues, and they wouldn't play that in a pub as Ulster-heavy as this one. The most popular song on the jukebox was Springsteen's "No Surrender".

As the bar got more crowded, Kevin tried buying his drinks two at a time. But the barmaid was on to him: she winked and said, "Your girlfriend drinking the same as you?" He wondered briefly if something in his face advertised that he was a loser. But a few more drinks made such thoughts go away. By midnight, he felt nothing at all. Past, present and future blurred into a slow cartoon of an eternal party. He was drinking in a way he never had before: not to feel but to stop feeling. Not to blur, but to obliterate. When a fight broke out and glasses were smashed on tables, some buried survival instinct prompted him to stagger towards the door.

A thin sleet was falling out of a starless sky. Kevin filled his lungs with cold night air, got no oxygen from it, tried again. He fell over the bonnet of a parked car and vomited painfully. When his vision cleared, he looked through the windscreen and saw a couple struggling together on the back seat. He looked away, pushed himself upright, and wiped his mouth. Then he saw a figure standing near the car park exit, watching him. It was Theresa.

She was wearing a pale blue jacket and skirt, not warm enough for standing outside. Her face was blank. There was no recognition in her eyes. As Kevin walked towards her, she didn't move. Close up, he could see that her face had a glassy sheen like a fresh scar. A car drove past outside, and he could just see its rear light through her. "Theresa," he said. Reached up and touched her cheek. His fingers were numb. "What happened to you?"

They stood like that for a few minutes. Then Kevin saw a pale trace of breath leave her mouth. Her throat trembled. He pulled her against him. When he kissed her, there was no sensation on his lips. "I'm sorry," he said. Slowly, she took hold of his hand. He felt the grip only as a paralysis, as if his muscles had seized up. Then she was pulling his arm, and they began to walk together into the flickering curtain of sleet.

For years, he'd told himself there was nothing to feel sorry for. Even now, it was the drink talking. They'd started going out together in the last year at school. It was his first relationship, but not hers. They'd been quite serious for a while, but Kevin had backed off from getting a place together. Let alone marriage, which was important to her. He'd kept thinking of his parents, how it had turned out between them. Theresa said the only way he could get away from his family was to start a new one. Gradually they'd begun to drift apart, then agreed to be friends.

He must have felt some resentment though. When Theresa had lost her job and was desperate for money, he'd introduced her to his mate Derek. At the time he'd told himself he was doing them both a favour, and it was her choice if anything happened. Derek made her an offer she couldn't refuse. He wasn't sure about the details, but a private party was involved. She'd never spoken to Kevin again.

Still holding hands, they walked slowly away from the main road and into the older part of the district. The remains of New Year parties were spilling out of pubs and houses as they passed. Kevin glimpsed shadows on either side: lads fighting in the street, couples locked together in doorways. The bassline of a Triangle song was shuddering through his head. He knew the way, though he couldn't have given anyone directions.

King's Standing Wood. They'd joked about the name as teenagers. It was a favourite spot for couples. He and Theresa had made love here a few times, that first spring they'd been together. More recently, the council had cut back a lot of the undergrowth to stop queers picking each other up here. They must have let it grow back, though: the paths were hidden now, and it was difficult to find a way through the black trees.

A few yards from the road, it was almost completely dark. Only the vague bluish glow of the city's light, reflected from the clouds overhead, made him able to see the trees. Beside him, Theresa was a walking shadow. The sleet had stopped falling, though the trees were dripping icy water. Kevin wanted to find a sheltered place where they could sit together. Just sit holding each other, and kiss, the way they used to. No more than that. He didn't know what she'd become. As long as her clothes stayed on, he could cope.

Something flapped past his head, a bird or a bat. On impulse, he put both his hands up to cover his face. When he reached back for Theresa, she wasn't there. He called her name, but there was no response. Then a shadow moved between the trees. He ran towards it, but no-one was there. A few steps further on, he glimpsed a blur of movement to one side. He cried out, lunged towards the shadow, tripped on a tree root, stumbled a few yards, struck a low branch with his forehead. Then he was on the ground, thorns tearing his numb hands, the stink of decaying leaves in his nose and mouth. The chill went for him and he curled up to escape it.

When he opened his eyes, a murky light was stirring beyond the trees. He looked at his watch, but the glass was cracked and he couldn't make out the time. His jacket and trousers were stained with mud. He struggled to his feet and shouted "Theresa?" No response. He rubbed his hands and blew into them, grateful when they began to ache.

By the time he reached the edge of the wood, he knew that some of last night had been vodka telling its stories. But perhaps Theresa, the real Theresa, had been with him. If so, was she still here? Had she hurt herself too? He walked back and forth through the trees and bushes, calling her name. Nothing stirred except a few birds, and a thin shape that could have been a dog or a fox.

Finally, he came to the toilets at the edge of the wood. They'd been boarded up for years, but now they were open. He checked the gents', almost passing out from the combined stink of bleach and rotting urine. Then, feeling awkward, he stepped into the ladies'. "Hello? Anyone there?" It was silent.

There was a different smell here, a worse one. Three cubicles and a cracked washbasin. Out of pure desperation, he pushed open the door of the first cubicle. There was dried blood on the cistern. Somehow he knew what he would see before he looked in the toilet bowl. It was curled up, safe in its own dream.

Kevin closed his eyes and stepped back. He felt shock and nausea building inside him, and knew he had to finish his search before they took control. Biting his lip, he opened the door of the second cubicle. Another twisted shape in the toilet bowl. A cold laugh twisted in his throat. He looked behind the third door. Another one, its face washed clean. He turned and ran out of the concrete building, kept running from street to street until the pain in his lungs forced him to stop.

He was on a canal bridge, somewhere north of the wood. There was no-one around. Frail light glittered on the frozen water. A dog ran along the towpath; it looked impossibly thin. Not far away, another dog was howling. In the street ahead, he could see an old train station with a wooden frontage. At once he knew what to do. People disappeared all the time, it wasn't so hard.

He bought a ticket to Stoke. That would do for a start. In the station toilets, he tried to clean some of the mud off his clothes. The sight of his own face in the rust-flecked mirror confused him. He didn't recognise himself. The face looked at least thirty, and there was grey stubble on its jaw. Well, that was another thing to leave behind. But it wasn't fair. He hadn't made anyone pregnant.

The train looked shabby, its paint scarred and faded. The interior was cold and smelt of diesel oil. But at least it wasn't a Virgin train. The carriage was empty and unlit.

Kevin sat by the window and watched the Black Country slip past. It looked wrong somehow. The buildings were too dark, prison-like hulks without windows or signs. The trees were strangely twisted, bony shapes crippled by the wind. The train passed a reservoir whose surface was perfectly black.

There didn't seem to be any stations. No-one came to check Kevin's ticket, and it was a long time before he took it out of his wallet and forced himself to read what was printed there.

All the Shadows

The hotel hasn't changed. Same tired-looking woman behind a reception desk cluttered with dusty paperwork. Same outdated optics behind the bar. Same obscure, faded pattern on the carpet. Same feeling that not only the air but the light has gone stale. I remember Nathan standing here, muttering to me: "This is a place where people come to die."

And here I am again, in the same hotel. Alone. I need to remember what happened, get it clear in my head by setting it down. If I can set it down. Memory is an infection: you can pass it on, but you can't get rid of it. Still, I need to pass the time somehow. I buy a drink at the bar, a vodka and cranberry juice. That's what Nathan used to drink. It seems important to remember him somehow. There are five men and two women scattered around the bar, all drinking alone. I don't feel like breaking the mould, but there are no free tables left. So I take my glass upstairs.

My room is on the second floor. It's smaller than the twin room I shared with Nathan, but has a similar look: old furniture probably bought at auction, wallpaper with a pattern of black seagulls, a carpet whose dull red texture hides a multitude of forensic. I sit at the low desk, open my little Silvine notebook and start writing. Which is how you get to read this. Hi. Don't worry, it doesn't go on for long.

We booked a twin room to be together without making it obvious. After all, this wasn't Brighton—though an hour walking along the coast would take us there. Nathan didn't like crowded places, said the traces were too changeable, he couldn't adjust. (I'll explain what he was talking about in a while.) So we went to quiet spots on holiday, which was all right as we mostly liked each other's company.

That afternoon in the hotel, we drew the curtains and put the twin beds together. It had been a long drive and we needed some downtime. In the half-light, Nathan looked like a ballet dancer: thin and pale, wrapped in his own stillness. We lay across the beds and grappled dreamily, biting without leaving marks. To avoid making a lot of noise, we curled together with our mouths on each other's cocks. The seagulls outside the window made more noise than we did. Afterwards, Nathan raised his head to look at me. There were tears in his eyes. "The last person to sleep here was a young woman," he said. "The other bed was empty. She went down to the beach in the night and drowned herself."

Nathan believed he was some kind of psychic sensitive. I was initially pretty sceptical, but went from seeing it as a dramatic pose to seeing it as a rather complex delusion that had to be treated sensitively. Later, I began to think he might be aware of subtle cues in the environment that pointed to things having gone wrong. When you're involved with someone, you can't ignore their hang-ups: you either start to share them or you fall out over them. After two years, I was getting more patient with his someone-died-here routine. But on this occasion, with the taste of his come still in my mouth, I turned away and muttered "For fuck's sake."

On our second date, we sat at an outdoor table in a Moseley pub garden. I went to the bar and came back with two pints of real ale. Nathan had gone very quiet. When he picked up his drink, I noticed his hand was shaking.

Then he shut his eyes and dropped his head onto his chest. I asked him what was wrong. After a few seconds, he opened his eyes. Another person was looking at me: a bitter, terrified child locked somewhere deep inside him. "There's blood on this table," he said. I looked down. "Not literally. Someone sat here last week who got hit by a car the next morning. He's dead."

Sometimes he'd change seats on a train or in a restaurant because he said it had "traces". More often he'd just sit and tremble, biting his lip, then slowly pull out of it. At my insistence, he went to the City Hospital for an EEG: I thought the episodes might be *petit mal* seizures. They didn't find any abnormality in his brain waves. I'd have thought the Trivium albums would show up somewhere.

The first time we went on holiday together, Nathan went into a trance in the shower of our Paris hotel room. I thought he was going to pass out. "The water tastes of blood," he said. "After a sleepless night, he cut his wrists. It took him hours to die." He was shivering so badly I had to help him dry himself. There were angry red marks on his wrists. Perhaps he'd scratched them when I wasn't looking. When he was calmer, I asked him why the man had died. "The police were closing in," Nathan said. "He'd strangled five children. They watched him die."

Sometimes he drew sketches of the people he'd "seen" dying. The sketches always showed faces just after death, looking blank and peaceful. I think that was his way of putting them to rest. Nathan worked as a designer for council publications: leaflets, manuals, reports. He was a talented artist, but the effort of concealing his "visions" and recovering from them had drained most of the energy from his working life. It wasn't always easy for me either. Sometimes I felt I was restoring Nathan's hope and vitality so that his ghosts could drain it, as if I was a blood donor and he was just a catheter, while the patient stood no chance of recovery.

That afternoon on the south coast, I was in no mood for another of Nathan's little dramas. So instead of nursing him through a quiet hour in the hotel, I insisted we get out to the beach while the sun was still bright. The streets were a pale film set, immaculate holiday cottages and retirement homes with no people in view. Seagulls flickered overhead like scratches in celluloid, screaming faintly. From the cliff edge, a steep path led down to a sheltered cove of blue-grey shingle. Where the cliff reached on either side, about fifty yards out, a single jagged rock poked from the water like a broken incisor tooth.

Oddly, given the fine weather, no-one else was there. The retreating tide had left a few yards of glistening stones and leathery strands of weed. A few black stains were probably jellyfish; I didn't feel like walking down to investigate. We spread out our towels on the dry upper shingle and stretched out to relax. I closed my eyes and stared into the blank daylight behind my eyelids.

But Nathan was restless. I heard him mutter: *So many feet on the stones. Hands reaching from the waves. Hair trailing back in the water. My God, how many people? Why were they never washed up on the beach? Why can't I see them properly? Shifting. Layers. Traces. How many times?* He was crying now. I opened my eyes to see him crouching on the towel, his hands crossed over his chest, rocking back and forth. It occurred to me that anyone who walked past would assume he was an addict.

"Nathan, what the fuck?" I reached for his arm. It was cold and wet, like part of a drowned man. He began to shake violently. I gripped him and held him down on the towel, firmly but without violence, until he was still. Not caring what any passers-by might think. Let them think the truth for fuck's sake. His eyes were dark with fear, but his lips were white. I felt something of my own inner being pass into him, and from him onto the stones of the beach. Leaving me empty, like a puppet he was manipulating to entertain an audience of the dead.

When he came back to himself, Nathan kissed me gently. "We have to get out of here," he said. "There's something I don't understand. So many dead people. Over and over. Like a record with so many overdubs you can't tell what's real. This part of the coast is a terrible place. We need to go."

"We're booked into the hotel," I said. "We can't afford to just pack up and leave. Why don't we stay in the hotel? We'll be safe there."

Nathan gazed at me. Mistrust and tenderness, anger and guilt were mixed up in his face. "What would I do without you?" he said. I couldn't answer, because at that precise moment I had no idea who I was. The blue-grey stones had taken it all. I wanted to cry, but the sun had dried out my skin. We stood up, folded our towels and walked back to the hotel. There was still no-one about.

It wasn't until the evening that all the others came. Not as a group: just one by one, drifting through the lobby, stopping at the bar for a glass of wine and a cigarette, taking their little overnight bags up the staircase. The lift was out of order. None of them spoke, which suggested they didn't know each other. None of them were using mobile phones. Apart from that, they could have been any solitary men and women on their way to somewhere. Just passing through.

Nathan wanted to go out for a meal. "I don't trust this place." We walked around the quiet streets for half an hour, but there were no restaurants and the only pub we found was closed for the night. There weren't even the usual fast-food places. The town was dead, but it wasn't decaying. There wasn't the damage, the neglect, the smell of despair that you find in districts where the future is missing. I'd grown up in a place like that. This town was different. It was just . . . not alive.

Perhaps that was why Nathan was in such an odd state of mind. He kept looking around nervously, as if expecting someone to appear. Every time a car went past, he flinched. "There's something wrong here," he said. "I can't feel any traces, but I know they're on everything. It's like trying to listen to the radio when all you can hear is static." Then he started telling me about his first psychic experience, when he was a child, but I made him stop. I wasn't in the mood.

Eventually we found an old fish and chip shop down by the seafront. The owner was a Chinese man in his seventies. I pictured him standing there night after night, telling himself that business would pick up some day, refusing to give up. Or was it just tonight that was like this? As he wrapped up our food, I asked him: "Why's it so quiet tonight?" He showed no sign of having heard me.

We ate our fish and chips walking past the seafront. The tide was coming in: dull water streamed between the upper rocks, almost reaching the wall. Out at sea there was some kind of turbulence: the surface was choppy, and mist and rain were shifting in the fading light. The fish was good, probably local, and wrapped in newspaper. I glanced at an oil-stained page and saw a date nearly ten years in the past. Of course, it was just a custom-made wrapping paper.

As we walked back to the hotel, the streetlights came on. Suddenly the town was rather beautiful in its stillness, like a pale sleeping face. I reached for Nathan's arm, and for a second we held each other. I could hear his breathing over the static of the distant waves. Our faces were close together. In that moment the silence of the town seemed natural, and seemed to be part of us.

There were more of the loners in the hotel bar. Nathan drank his vodka and cranberry a little too fast, and was stumbling on the narrow staircase. We lay down on our twin beds. He started to tell me again about his first psychic experience, and this time I didn't stop him. *I was in hospital after having my tonsils out. Kept spitting blood, but it didn't hurt, I must have been on painkillers. They gave me soup all the time. Tomato soup. Never liked it since. My mother came to visit me every day. She and my dad were starting to fall out. I was lonely on the ward, but I secretly hoped they'd keep me there forever, so I didn't have to be at home with the arguments or go to school with the other kids picking on me. I was nine.*

There was a rocking horse on the ward. One evening I got up and went to sit on it. Didn't expect it to move, but it did. I rocked it back and forth very slowly, so it wouldn't creak and bother the nurses. Then I saw a boy on the horse, just where I was. His head flew back, and he started coughing blood. It was all over him, over the horse, the floor. He fell off and twisted on the ground. His face was dead white. People were running and shouting. I let the horse stop rocking, got off it and went back to my bed. The next day I told my mother I wanted to go home.

Nathan stopped. I kissed him gently. We moved together, just touching. He rested his head on my chest. Then he looked up. "Jesus wept," he said, then went over to the window. We hadn't shut the curtains. "How many of them?" I could see his pale hand on the glass, shaking. I got up to join him.

The street was flooded with people, all walking down towards the shore. They looked like the people we'd seen in the hotel. Loners, people on the way through. Some had coats and scarves, but none of them were carrying any luggage. "Where are they going?" I asked.

Nathan looked at me. His face was a mask of fear. "I don't know. Or where they've come from. We'd better stay in here." He pulled the curtain shut. But I was already making for the door. He followed me along the half-lit corridor and down the stairs, not speaking. I felt his hand pull at my sleeve, but I couldn't stop. Other people were coming out of their rooms, going down to the hotel lobby. They seemed to know what was happening. I followed them.

When we got to the cliff edge and looked down over the shingle beach, I saw it was already full of people. None of them touched or looked at each other. They were all staring out to sea. The storm was closer: black waves rose and clawed at the misty air. It was starting to rain. We joined the line of people walking down the steep wooden steps. I thought of my father, who'd climbed the stairs at home only to collapse in the dark hallway, his bed forever beyond reach.

Around us, people were stepping forward, their feet slipping on the wet stones. Some of them fell and got up again. As the storm broke and rain tore through the open door of the night, those nearest the water began to move forward. Nathan caught my hand. "Help me," he said. "I don't want to drown. They're trying to make me join them. We have to go back." I raised his stiff hand to my lips. The black water didn't seem cold at all. Just ahead, I could see their heads bobbing on the restless surface. Some of them went under. I felt Nathan's hand still pulling at me, trying to make me stop. I let go.

He didn't follow me out past the jagged rock. He couldn't swim.

Neither could I.

Some of the faces in the hotel bar look familiar. Maybe I've seen them here before. But the one I always hope to see is never here. Maybe his visions helped him to keep going after all. Why should he join me, when I wouldn't stay for him? All I have here is the memory of his voice, his hands on me, the taste of his sperm. And the strangers who join me here. They don't speak to me, and I don't speak to them. There are a few more of them every year.

Maybe we're all hoping that by coming back, we'll go on recruiting until the people we want are here. Like some political group that's convinced its time will come, no matter how little changes. Or maybe the reason we come back is just that we don't want to die alone. But somehow, every time, we do.

Midnight Flight

Paul Cooksey remembered the book's title on the same day that he forgot where he lived. As his bus neared the Hockley Flyover and the tall buildings on either side receded, he had a momentary sensation of flying on wings of concrete. Night was falling, but the streetlamps hadn't yet come on. Cars streamed past on the outside lane. He closed his eyes, and a name he'd been trying to recall for months came back to him as naturally as if he'd never lost it. *Midnight Flight.*

The editor's name continued to elude him, and it wasn't any of the usual suspects. The book had been in the school library, quite battered when he'd read it in . . . 1966 it must have been, when he was twelve. The first book of horror stories he'd read, unless you counted the children's versions of Norse and Greek myths and *Beowulf,* which you probably should.

As the bus crawled through heavy traffic on the Soho Road, the teenagers shouting into their mobiles and headphones leaking beats drove the book from his mind. But now he'd remembered the title, maybe he'd be able to track down a copy. It might even have the original cover. He couldn't see through the murky windows to identify his stop, and the chanting around him was getting louder as if the reception was better at this point. Paul rose to his feet and cautiously pushed his thin body past the standing youngsters. Nobody moved to let him through.

Midnight Flight. There was a story about a lonely boy who collected moths and was drained of blood by a vengeful giant moth with skulls on its wings. And a story about a dead lake haunted by a terrible black moth. There were other kinds of winged creatures in the book, including one that could only fly in utter darkness because it came from outer space, but it was the moth ones he remembered most clearly. For years he'd dreamt of flying through the night on fragile wings.

"Get out the fucking way!" A boy on a racing bike narrowly missed him on the pavement. The cold air transmitted the near-impact. Paul looked around in confusion. He must have taken a wrong turning: there were no familiar landmarks in sight. A woman with a pram was approaching; he'd better ask her.

"Excuse me," he said as she drew level with him. "Do you know the way to . . . " *What was the name of the road?* He shook his head. "Shit."

"Even my daughter knows that." The woman smiled. "Where are you trying to get to?"

"My flat. Just can't . . . " Blood rose to his face, silencing him.

"Have you got a bus pass?"

"I can walk, it's not far." Though he was no longer sure of that.

The woman touched his arm. "For your address."

Doubtful, Paul pulled out his wallet and checked. His address in Victoria Road was there. He'd never been good with women's names. "Thank you," he said, breathless with relief.

"No worries." He watched her continue up the road, weaving to negotiate the shattered paving-stones. The sky overhead was fully dark; a helicopter's light moved slowly above the rooftops. Paul replaced his wallet and buttoned up his coat. He wasn't convinced the face in the bus pass photo was him, but you couldn't be sure of everything.

Three days later, he remembered the editor's name. It happened in the Black Eagle, while he was trying to read the new menu. The lines were too close together, blurring like ripples on still water. He folded the card and put it down, trying to recall what he'd last eaten here. At the next table, a middle-aged man with a beard was being tugged from side to side by headphones plugged into some round, black device that looked about to crawl away. He raised his arms above his head. Paul looked back down at the menu card and immediately saw the words: *Thom Creighton Parr.* He adjusted his glasses and read: *Torn chicken pasta.* But he was sure it was the right name. When he closed his eyes he could see it under the book's title, superimposed on an image of blurred wings against the night. Black on dark blue.

The pasta was too expensive, so he opted for pie and chips, which didn't remind him of anything. It didn't taste of anything either. The bearded man played invisible drums in the air. The sound of voices arguing at another table rose to a violent pitch, though Paul couldn't see any movement. He left his pint unfinished. On the way out, a grey-haired woman turned her head towards him and smiled. "How's it going?" He didn't recognise her; she must be speaking to someone else. But she looked disappointed when he didn't stop. Embarrassment made him head for the door as quickly as his shaky legs would go. Was it possible that every memory he regained had to be paid for with another one?

A grey dawn was filtering through the curtains, turning his bed to concrete. Paul sat up and gripped the sides of his head to absorb the dull throbbing before it could break free. His throat was dry. Flakes of dead skin drifted from his fingertips. Was that what old age meant, that the layers of skin went deeper so that less and less of you was alive? He reached out to the bedside table, switched on the lamp and picked up a second-hand book. A detective story. But his eyes were too tired: the lines of print crept across the yellowing paper. When he couldn't read, why was he convinced that *Midnight Flight* would release him from pain and loneliness? Was it just because it had done that for him as a child?

Perhaps the local library could help him. Not that it would have the book, or any book published in the last century. But the computers whose blank screens had frozen him out might hold some answers. Paul washed and dressed a little faster than his usual lethargic morning pace, putting on his favourite cardigan despite the holes he noticed in its left shoulder and arm. *Midnight Flight* was out there, nestling on a wooden shelf, its pages waiting to be turned again. Maybe the same copy he'd read and re-read all those years ago.

The library's few bookshelves were mostly taken up with standard reference works and large print volumes—which Paul, for the first time, wondered if he ought to borrow one of. A few newspapers were scattered on the tables between the long ranks of computers.

The librarian, a short middle-aged man with an oddly boyish expression, looked up *Midnight Flight* on his desk terminal. "No copies in the library system any more," he said. "There'd be one at the British Library, of course, but that's in London. Have you tried ABE Books?" He didn't know what that was. The librarian checked his ticket, then found him a computer and showed him how to search. No second-hand copy seemed to be available online. The librarian left him to further searches. "Good luck, Mr.

Cooksey." Paul wondered who he was talking to. He had to look back at his own ticket to see that was his name.

A search for Thom Creighton Parr yielded seven links. Three of them were to listings of second-hand copies of his book on bowling, *Green Pastures*, while two more were bowling society websites that cited the same book. Another was a Wikipedia entry that gave Parr's birth date as 1923, but no death date. It mentioned *Midnight Flight*, but only to describe it as a "long-forgotten horror anthology" with only one edition, in 1964.

The final link was to a website called Crypt of Cobwebs, dedicated to British and American horror fiction. Paul hadn't read much in that genre since *Midnight Flight*. He'd tried a few other anthologies in the sixties and seventies but had given up, nauseated by severed heads and vats of acid. The linked passage was in an article on British horror anthologies before 1980. It said:

> *One of weird fiction's great "lost books" is* Midnight Flight *edited by Thom Creighton Parr (Acheron Press, 1964), which is thought to have included tales by Lovecraft and Jacobi. All the stories involve winged nocturnal creatures. A reviewer called the book "too disturbing to read", and it was never reprinted— though of course, true weird fiction stood little chance of being appreciated in the Marxist sixties. Copies are hard to track down. It's rumoured that copyright problems led to copies of the book being recalled. Or maybe they just flew away.*

The article was by Niall Verde. Working back through the Crypt's elaborate structure, which seemed to extend under a broad church, Paul found topics ranging from an early Gothic novel to a recent erotic vampire thriller. Verde was among the most frequent posters. His comments, always made in the early hours of the morning, were mostly concerned with how little "the herd" understood about "true weird fiction". In the course of a bitter argument with another insomniac, he remarked that "visionary" works such as his own collection *The Veil of Fail* were doomed to oblivion because "writers who care more about creating great fiction than self-promotion will always be passed over." There was a link to Verde's personal website, but Paul had seen enough. He cleared the screen, then tried a search for Acheron Press. Much to his surprise, the imprint still existed. He wrote down the address, which was in Stafford.

The train shuddered as it lost and gained speed, pausing between stations in a landscape of shut-down factories and empty fields. The view had been sprayed white and called morning, but he could see the night sky underneath. Then the young man sitting in front of him pulled down the grey curtain so he could read his phone. Paul closed his eyes and shivered. He didn't want to be alone with his memories, because they couldn't be relied on. The gaps were spreading, a ragged pattern of darkness like the wings on the cover of *Midnight Flight*.

He'd written to Acheron Press, and a typed letter had come back with a shaky signature. The original publisher was still alive, though a decade older than Paul, and said he still got occasional queries about *Midnight Flight*. Their stock had been destroyed in a fire in 1971. There'd been some ex-library copies in circulation for a while. They'd never considered reprinting the book because, after the fire, they'd switched to publishing non-fiction—mostly natural history and Egyptology. The business was steadily winding down, though a few local societies and museums supported it.

What had made Paul buy the train ticket was the news that Parr was still alive. The Acheron publisher still sent him occasional royalties for some entomology books he'd provided photographs for. Since 2006 he'd been living at a nursing-home in Stoke-on Trent. The publisher had commented: "He and I used to keep in touch, but these days I'm afraid he's hardly there."

The train ground to a halt. Paul wiped his eyes with a hand that felt dry as paper. Surely this was the fool's errand to end them all. A man losing his memory on a quest to find a man who'd already lost his own. He wanted to believe that Parr could help him find the book—or even tell him, from further down the road, where his own journey into darkness was heading. Perhaps this happened to everyone who'd read the book.

Last night he'd sat by the phone, trying to remember his sister's number or the number of anyone he knew. His address book had flown away months ago. Paul had lived alone since his teens. Hadn't slept with a woman in thirty years, still missed it though he doubted much would happen if he got the chance. All in all, he'd rather miss things than forget what they were like. Hence the ticket. . . .

On the platform at Stoke, Paul was surprised how unsteady his legs were. As if not just the two-hour journey but the change of scene had affected his connection with the ground. He bought an A-Z map in the station newsagent, but couldn't make out the street names. Outside the station, everywhere seemed to be boarded up. He'd never find the way. It was hard enough with places he knew. Behind the derelict buildings, the illusion of daylight seemed more fragile than ever. He waved down a black cab and asked the driver for the Tyton Retirement Home.

"Been away, have you?" the driver asked as Paul settled himself awkwardly in the back.

"Yes." Why not let him think that? If he said he didn't live here, there would be questions he couldn't answer. The cab swerved around potholes in the road, passed the grey skeletons of buildings. This might as well be his home: a town that had lost its sense of identity. He belonged here. The driver stopped at a traffic light; a young woman crossed the road, a phone pressed to the side of her face.

The nursing-home was a few miles out of town, where the dereliction was softened by the flame and rust of autumn trees. Dead leaves marked the road with an incomplete pattern. The cab's wheels crunched on the gravel driveway. The building had a new white frontage, though its side was rotting grey brick. Paul paid the driver; it was almost all the cash he had.

The young male nurse who answered the door stared at Paul as if trying to remember who he was. Paul knew how the lad felt. He said, "I've come to visit Mr. Parr. Is he in?"

The nurse nodded. "You'll find him in room seventeen, ground floor." As Paul moved towards the door, he added: "Have you booked?"

"Sorry, no. I wasn't sure when I'd get here." The nurse looked like he was considering blocking the way, but then stepped aside at the last moment.

The interior of the home was poorly lit and smelt like an old-fashioned dry cleaner. Mothballs, that was it. Pipes vibrated behind the walls. The dirt in the cracked floor-tiles suggested a partly-erased image. Most of the doors were shut, but the open ones leaked other smells: antiseptic, stale urine, bacon. A cry echoed through the narrow corridor, more like a seagull than a human voice.

Room 17 was on the right, a long way into the building. Paul had to touch the raised number to make sure of it. The door was open by a crack. He pressed his shoulder to it and stepped through. A small room with a table and a few chairs, a bookcase, a TV set with the picture on but no sound. A flickering mercury light. Two shrunken figures in armchairs, not watching the TV. Neither of them moved as Paul entered the room.

"Is Thom Parr in here?"

The two men looked at each other. Then one of them pointed back over his shoulder. Paul realised there was a side room, or an alcove, with a vague shape just visible against a creased black curtain. "Thank you," he said, and walked though. The stuttering of the light made it hard to understand what was there. The curtain was just random streaks of damp in the wall. The man seated in the chair, or rather held by it in a sitting position, was wrapped below the neck in a lace blanket. He was almost bald. His eyes were sunk so far into his narrow face that it took Paul a while to see that they were open.

"Mr. Parr? Hello?" The face didn't stir. Paul looked closer. He could have been looking in a cracked and grimy mirror. "I'm a reader," he said, and blushed with shame at the uselessness of that. "Are you okay?"

There was no sound of breath. The old man's lips trembled, but perhaps that was just the light. Paul reached out slowly and touched the side of his throat, where the pulse should be. The flesh was cold. He brushed a fingertip against the dry lips: no air movement. He wondered what he might have to do to be sure that Parr was dead. Maybe the problem was in himself.

He reported the death back at the reception desk. They didn't seem either surprised or upset. He asked if there was anyone who needed to be informed, and was told that Parr had no relatives and no property. Everything he owned had been sold to pay for his place at the retirement home.

When Paul left, the daylight was fading. He felt drained by the effort of reporting the death, as if he'd used up his clarity of mind for the day. He'd better get back to the station, but that didn't seem possible until he got his bearings. The still face drifted in front of him, shedding flakes of skin like dead leaves. His legs ached, but he couldn't stop walking until the white building was out of sight. Then he walked on, looking for a sign.

Woodland, reminding him of childhood walks with his parents. Later, with girlfriends, he'd stayed in the city, maybe walked hand in hand along the canal towpath. Never made love out-of-doors. But the smell of decaying leaves excited him for some reason he couldn't explain. If only he could find the book, he could become Parr, not have to go home to a city he didn't know any more.

Not only his legs but his lungs ached, his hands were losing sensation, his throat was raw. But he couldn't stop. As if there were wings at his back. Night was falling, crossing out the errors of daylight. Burning the page. At the edge of the wood, he reached a derelict house. Its doorway and windows were boarded up. Had Parr tried to sell it? He dimly remembered going into a derelict house on one of those childhood walks, finding a butterfly brooch, giving it to his mother. Black or dark blue. Had that happened, or was it a dream?

Behind the house was a patch of wasteground. He couldn't see where it ended, though he could hear running water. And a faint pulse, like the beating of wings. He could just make out a few dead trees in the half-light around him, with no leaves to shed. Had this been a garden? Was his real life coming to an end, as well as the false life in a city whose name he couldn't remember? The ground was as cold as the thin face he'd touched. The pulsing of wings made him flatten himself against the dead grass and fragments of stone, the pattern he couldn't see.

Then the wings were above him, beating slowly in the dark, their edges brushing his face. The pages turning. The dark covers shutting out the town's distant light. A clear memory came back to him: lying with his first girlfriend on a narrow bed, pinning back her wings of flesh with his tongue. Their hands locked together. And then the book folded around his body, and its dry pages gave the dust of their stories back to him.

Ashes in the Water

with Mat Joiner

The canal walkway looked colder than it was. Boarded-up factory windows, coils of razor-wire, gaunt bridges, blackened leaves on the path. But the still air was dense with traffic fumes, warm enough to make Josh sweat under his winter coat. After dark, the only light came from the distant streetlamps; it turned the view to a sketch, more remembered than seen. He'd known this stretch of the Grand Union Canal for thirty years; it never seemed to change. Maybe that was why Anthony had come to live here. The peace of abandoned things was better than no peace at all.

A bin liner swollen with rubbish or gas was floating just below the water surface. Broken glass crunched under Josh's feet. He glanced around nervously; there was no-one in sight. Beyond the next bridge, he could just make out the thin black silhouette of a narrowboat. Was that the right one? They were hard to tell apart in such poor light. The rotting stone of the bridge was another thing that took him back to the past. Buildings decayed, but not on a human timescale. There were lights on the boat. He could see its painted name: *Eyewitness*.

When he knocked on the barely visible door, it opened. Anthony looked older than before, though that could be just the light. He gripped Josh's hand. "Welcome! Come aboard." Josh hesitated, thinking of the ribbon of black water between him and the boat. Anthony smiled and tugged his arm, pulling him through the doorway and into the sanctuary he'd created for himself after a summer of madness.

The small room had a central table, two wooden chairs and a few small bookcases. Some of Anthony's old stuff was here: second-hand books of poetry, politics and occultism. But the table was covered with atlases and maps Josh hadn't seen before. Other maps were stuck to the walls; they looked too old to be of any practical use. They sat down, and Anthony poured them both a glass of wine. "Good to see you," he said.

"And you. The boat's great. Do you stay in the same place, or move around from time to time?"

"I could move if I wanted to. But there's no reason. I like sleeping on water. Makes me feel more connected somehow. Do you think I'm still mad?"

Josh remembered Anthony in hospital, the stitched gashes in his wrists, the random comments about nobody meaning what they said. Being forced out of his job, breaking up with his wife, and then being unable to sleep—ordinary pressures that had driven him into a strange place. He'd seemed obsessed with the difficulty of knowing what was real and what was imagined. The issue of trust. It was odd how people in their forties often lost faith in their own maturity and decided to step backwards. Josh supposed he had that to look forward to.

"No," he said. "You're a bit troubled I suppose. Like most of us. But if living here makes you feel more sure of things, that's a start."

"You can't really be sure of anything. Cheers, pal." They raised their glasses. The wine had a smoky aftertaste. Anthony raised his arms, stretching in his chair. "Excuse me. I've been on my feet most of today. My back's playing up."

"Where you been?"

"Took the day off work, walked up the canal about ten miles past Solihull. Thinking about what it was like before the war. When they joined up the waterways between London and Birmingham to let trade through. You walk around this area now, you can see the effect of destroying industry. Leaving people with nothing real to hold onto. But it happened to the canals a generation before.

"What *are* the canals, do you think? A bit of random heritage, a scar tissue under the roads? A hidden place for drunks and drug addicts and teenage couples and gay leathermen? I can tell you it's more than that. It's a palimpsest. A map of industry . . . and beneath that, the key to another world."

Josh thought of Anthony in school: the Crowley and Castaneda books, the Tarot cards, all the scraps of folk-religion the boy had used to compensate for the disintegration of his family. Josh had tried to become a follower, but only because he'd wanted to get close to Anthony. That was all history now: they'd resolved the issue back in their twenties. Now Anthony had reverted to his mysticism. Would Josh go back to the torment of isolation? He drained his glass with a quiet spasm of grief. "What's wrong?" Anthony asked.

"It's all right. Just . . . it's Warren. He's been having trouble breathing. They found a tumour in his throat. He's having radiotherapy. The doctor told him he'd got a fifty per cent chance. His reaction was, 'Thanks for being honest.' He won't say he's frightened, but sometimes he cries in his sleep." The room was blurring.

"My God, I'm sorry. That's terrible." Josh and Warren had been together for nine years, and sharing a house for the last five years. Anthony refilled their glasses. "You know, it's how you feel about someone being really ill that tells you whether you love them. Not whether you enjoy sex with them. Or whether you're faithful to them. The threat of death takes you to the heart of it."

Josh sipped the dark wine. "What do you mean, another world?"

Anthony paused, winding back through the conversation. He'd always had an analogue mind where Josh was digital.

"If I knew what I meant, I'd use different words," he said at last. "The canal system is a kind of language. It's like scarring—a symbolic message written by real events. It's neither one thing nor the other. Living here means I have one foot in the real world and one . . . somewhere else. In the realm of vision."

Maybe his first question had been to the point: he was still mad. But "mad" only meant not coping, and he was coping. Josh drank some more wine and looked at the half-lit room: the maps, the books, the 1980s records. The thin, balding friend he'd once desired with a passion, but now viewed with unconflicted respect. Maybe there was something to be said for growing up.

Through the walls of the narrowboat, he could smell the decay held in the body of still water. They weren't far from the traffic on the Warwick Road, but even so Josh felt encased in a silence that was more than physical. It occurred to him that the boat was a kind of coffin—or rather, a sarcophagus.

The funeral was a bastard. Josh had worked closely with Warren's family and some of his old friends to get the details right. To choose some pieces of music ("Wichita Lineman" and "Hour of Darkness") that had mattered to Warren. To make some kind of meaningful statement about his life in the narrow time-slot offered by the crematorium. The humanist who conducted the funeral was a decent guy who took time to understand who Warren had been, and to help make sure the ceremony had meaning and dignity. But it was still a bastard.

Dust blew through the silences, mould streaked the pale casket. Every note was played on a string over a bottomless abyss. At the reception, Josh drank heavily without feeling a breath lighter or more human. *This is the real world,* he thought. *The life you thought you had was just a film. Behind the screen, there's this.* Later, some of their friends came back to the house for a wake. That was worse.

Three nights later, Josh walked out along the Grand Union Canal. There was frost on the ground, and a faint smell of burning in the cold air. His lack of sleep made the view seem unreal, a child's black paper cut-out with painted stars. The barking of a dog echoed from the backs of factories. Dead leaves were floating on the water. A young man walked past, his face a mask of scar tissue.

There was the old bridge with its odour of rotting brick. And beyond, the black narrowboat. There were no lights on it. Probably Anthony was out. But he knocked. No answer. He was turning away when the door slowly opened. A thin face looked out from the unlit doorway: a very old woman. "Hello?" she said. "Who's there?" He wasn't sure she could see him.

"I'm sorry. I must have the wrong boat. I'm a friend of Anthony Walker."

"Josh, isn't it?" Was she Anthony's mother? "You'd better come on board." She reached behind her head and switched on a light.

The room looked nothing like his friend's. There were no books, no pictures. Only hanging cloths and some carvings that might be bone or ivory. The old woman turned her wrinkled face towards him. Cataracts had filled her eyes with milk. "If you want to talk to him, I can help you," she said.

"To Anthony? Where is he?" She paused, then shook her head. He realised what she was talking about. "I don't believe in that."

"So why have you come here? It wasn't a mistake." Her voice was hollow with pain. Something had taken her life away and left her nothing but a sketch, an echo-chamber. The lines in her face were a map. "This boat is like a brothel. People only come here for one reason."

Josh bit his lip. The table between them was covered with scraps of fabric that looked and smelt like dead leaves. The words left his mouth before he had thought them. "Where is he?"

"On the canal. I can hear him through water, the vibrations." Her face twisted, and she grasped at her shoulders as if pulling down an invisible scarf over her black housecoat. Suddenly her mouth opened and a sound came out. It wasn't a voice. Josh felt sick. He imagined a dead man in the water using the old woman as a dummy. But when he tried to turn away, he couldn't move.

Out of the jagged wound of her mouth came a baby's fragile cry. The chaotic babble of a toddler. The nagging voice of a child, deepening into the rasp of an adolescent. Words flowing together so fast, rippling and blurring, he couldn't make anything out. Then, suddenly, Warren. "Don't let go of me." His voice reduced to a hoarse whisper by surgery. "Don't let go of me."

Before he could say it again, Josh made for the door, pulled it open and jumped onto the bank. His hands and face felt as cold as snow. Trembling violently, he staggered to the bridge and crouched there. He wanted to vomit, but only clear water trickled from his mouth. From the canal, or from his memory, he could just make out the same words. *Don't let go of me.* He bit his knuckles until he tasted blood. It wasn't warm.

Another night, the same winter. He was standing on a towpath he didn't know. His shoes were caked with mud, so he must have walked miles, but he couldn't remember the journey. Behind him was the dull throat of a bridge. Willows laced the twilight sky. The canal whispered, reflecting nothing.

Then the bridge gave birth: a sharp prow cut the water, and the boat was there. A wide barge, rather old-fashioned in design. Streaked with algae, ridged here and there with some dull metal. Its lanterns were unlit, but there was a moon. The barge passed him, and he saw its crew.

Their skin glimmered without any colour. Shadows suggested clothes and eyes, but he didn't know if they could see him. They were quite still; only their outlines flickered. He thought, *Anthony.* He wasn't sure his friend was on board. But Anthony should know about this. So he walked after the barge.

He couldn't quite keep level with it. Sometimes he lagged behind, other times he was ahead. Its engines were silent, though after a while he could hear the voices of the crew. They came to him as ripples, breaking bubbles: nothing he could make sense of. The barge was nudging through a thicket of weeds when he realised he was seeing the passengers, not the crew.

Ahead was a light: a human-shaped glimmer among the bushes on the towpath. Its outlines were blurred, as if drawn on tracing paper. The boat drew level with it, slowed enough for the image to drift over the water and settle on deck. The others shifted to accommodate it, but that was the only welcome it got.

Perhaps Anthony wasn't there. He was looking for someone else now—but the faces of the passengers waned and swam, defying focus. He called out: *Warren?* Was that a reply trailing in the barge's wake? The moon was gone: he could only see by the passengers. He thought there was another traveller ahead, but the pale stirring was an open lock. The water beyond churned silently.

He had a few moments' view of the landscape beyond, a sprawl of black shapes. Cairns or houses? Slow grey sparks tracked between them. Dead stars or drifting souls? He had no time to decide: the lock was closing, the barge had slipped away, and now everything was lost in an ordinary darkness.

If he couldn't find the barge awake, maybe he could dream it back from its moorings in the dark world. It would never be without passengers. All he had to do was wait by the canal. Something natural and quiet: an old heart stuttering in the night. Nothing violent. He lay in bed and formed the elements—water, trees, dusk—in his mind. It was easy to return, more digital than analogue. Now on a bridge, now on the edge of the towpath. Leaves, dark birds, ordinary narrowboats drifted by.

Was there some kind of law? You only saw the barge twice: once in dreams, then when you were ready to board. He doubted you could get a return ticket. What was he supposed to do?

One night (the dream placed him in a winter afternoon, light smeared on a dove-grey sky), he was staring down at the flawed skin of the canal. It looked solid, but it would be easy to break. He swung himself over the side of the bridge. He would swim to the dark land. The distance didn't bother him.

The chill of the water did. He went under in a moment, weed snagging his ankles. The sun fractured in waves, went out. Somehow he found his way back to the air and clutched at an overhanging branch. There was no way he could swim in this. It was an abyss. Then he realised how he could find the barge.

It was easier than he could have imagined, once he'd made the choice. He laughed and felt his last breath rise free. He was flooding, lungs and then veins, his body turning into a maze of canals. There was a silt-green dusk. Then night, but not as black as the world beyond the locks.

He was wondering when he'd reach bottom, and if he'd see the barge from that far down, when he woke. Still dead. There was a veil on his face, and his shroud was wet through. He cried out, ripped the weed from his eyes, kicked the sheets away. They were rank and sodden. When he turned on the light, he saw dark water pooling on the floor. There was mud in it, dead leaves, God knew what.

He might be staggering away from the towpath. He might be lying still in murky water. Feeling lost, he groped his way to the bathroom and was sick again and again. Only when he'd coughed out the last of it did he know he was at home. The thought brought him no comfort. It couldn't, not any more.

The hospital made him think of Warren's last days. *Don't let go of me.* But there were no ghosts here. It was too far from the canal. Only the machines flickered, only the slow red drip from the hanging plastic bag flowed. The air was dry and warm. He'd managed to call an ambulance before the blood infection took hold. It had its own sweet lonely call, like a drug, pulling him down into nothing. But he didn't trust its voice. He didn't trust the spirit medium. He didn't trust.

But Anthony's visit was a surprise. He'd come from work, wearing a black suit. *It's not my funeral yet,* Josh thought. There was strength in the thin man's hand. "What have you done to yourself?"

"Don't know," Josh said. "Wasn't suicide. I got ill. Too much time outdoors. Was going mad." Had Anthony been through something similar? He looked up into his friend's tired face, hoping for a sign. "You were right," he said. "The canal is the real world."

Anthony almost smiled. "There is no real world. But any kind of peace is worth holding onto. Look, Josh—would you like to come and stay with me for a bit? There's more space on my boat than you'd think, there's a spare bedroom. It might help you. Just for a few weeks, a break, you'd be welcome."

Josh closed his eyes and listened to Anthony's calm voice. "No phone, no broadband. Just a world of peace and stillness. Part of the landscape, but not caught up in it. The hidden core. It might be what you need. It saved me."

"I'll think about it." Then a nurse came to check Josh's tubes. He was still feverish; the sheets were damp with sweat. Anthony gripped his hand again, then stood up and waved goodbye. It was early evening. Josh felt so tired he wondered how he'd ever kept awake. In his mind, the black flakes were still drifting. He'd never seen the fire.

The sky was an old bruise, swollen with rain. Josh had walked out from the crowded city centre to the older Digbeth streets above the canal. It had been a month, but seemed much longer; he had some trouble finding the steps. Eventually he was standing on the towpath. The dead leaves had washed away. There were still burnt-out fireworks in the water from November. He looked to the south, away from the city. The backs of disused factories were just visible in the twilight.

He was carrying a travel bag with a few necessities, enough to see him through the weekend. If it worked out, he'd go back for more clothes. And he'd had to leave space in the bag for what the funeral parlour had given him. There hadn't been a right time, never would be. He thought: *If not now, when?*

Some distance further up the canal, past a misshapen bridge and a wall sprayed with graffiti tags, a few trees were reaching over the water. Josh stood there for a while. He thought of Warren: not in hospital, white and voiceless, but as he'd been when they'd first got together. Sitting with him in a pub garden, drinking wine, their hands gesturing in conversation and touching as if by accident. He unzipped his travel bag and took out the grey plastic urn. It was surprisingly heavy.

As night fell, Josh walked on beyond the trees, under another bridge, past another factory with bricked-up windows. He swung the urn over the dull water, trailing ashes like strands of blackened tissue. A nursery rhyme, barely remembered, played over and over in his head:

Ashes in the water
Ashes in the sea
We all jump up
With a one, two, three

Finally, the plastic container was empty. He sealed it and put it back in the travel bag. Then he walked on. There was no moon, but the clouds and traffic fumes held the city's light like a dusty crystal ball. In the distance, he could make out the long black shape of a narrowboat. He hoped it was the right one.

For Their Own Ends

Barry's walk home from the library nearly took him to the crematorium, though that was miles out of his way. It was a hot day, and dust was shimmering above the crowded road. Something he'd read in the papers had disturbed him—afterwards, he couldn't recall what. When the air suddenly felt too dense to breathe, he assumed that was another effect of his mood. The pain spreading across his chest to his left arm was obviously indigestion brought on by eating his breakfast too quickly, eager to get out of the house. When a few people gathered around him to ask if he was all right, Barry wanted to say that he was fine, they didn't have to worry. But he had no voice.

He could feel a distant shuddering in the ground, like traffic going past. The air smelt faintly of disinfectant. Close by, a woman's voice was saying: "I can't turn it on unless you pay up front. Do you have a credit card?" He was in a long, dusty room with grey-painted walls and mercury strip lights, one of which was flickering. People were lying motionless on narrow beds. Each bed had a TV beside it. That was what the nurse was talking about, he realised as she walked past in a light grey uniform. The patient she'd been talking to was lying on his side, facing Barry. His mouth was open, but he wasn't speaking. The only sound was the stuttering of the defective mercury light.

His life felt like a dream that he'd woken up from to this. It had been coming on for a while, he realised. Ever since those final weeks at work—the "restructuring" that had seen most of the decent people, including management, forced out to make room for the new MD's friends. Those long, futile union meetings, trying to save jobs when no agreement to protect them was in place. The blank expression of the HR manager, like someone trying not to be sick. The terrible one-to-one meetings with union members who saw their jobs being swept away. He'd started to get shortness of breath, blurred vision, even momentary blackouts. The symptoms had just seemed a natural part of what was happening. Losing his own job had been almost a relief, given how things had broken down. At least he wouldn't have to go on hearing the MD say, "Change is the norm."

Some time later, the same nurse walked past again. She noticed Barry was awake and smiled at him. "Glad you're back with us." She felt his pulse, touched his forehead, then jotted something on a clipboard. "The doctor will be here soon. You've had a heart attack. We tried to contact your next of kin, but the number was unobtainable." Barry realised they probably still had his father's number. He had no family left in this country. "How are you feeling?"

"Not too bad. How long have I been here?" His voice sounded thin, like a bootleg copy of itself. But at least it didn't take his breath with it. There was a dull ache in his chest, like a lost tooth.

"About four hours," the nurse said. "Just take it easy. I'm going to give you some medication." She took a syringe out of a metal case, tied up Barry's left arm and injected a clear fluid into it. He didn't feel anything. "That should help keep your heartbeat stable for a few hours. If you have any problems, let us know." She glanced at her watch, looking anxious, and moved on.

The drug had no immediate effect. Was he going to need that just to remain in a normal state? An hour or so passed by, and the light coming through the murky windows began to fade. None of the patients appeared to be conscious, but Barry could hear someone not far away struggling to breathe, as if in pain.

A bent old man in a charcoal-grey suit, holding a thin PDA, walked slowly past and paused at each bed to gaze at its occupant. Was he the doctor? He looked more like a patient, apart from his outfit. When he reached Barry, he tapped something into the PDA. Barry had the strange impression that the old man's skin was coated with ashes.

Two young women came round to take dinner orders. Their white shirts had identical red and black logos. One of them gave Barry a printed menu: under the heading Hospital-ity Inc. was a list of available dishes with prices. "Beans on toast is free," she said. "Other options are reasonably priced." Barry asked for some toast without beans. "I'm not sure they can do that. I'll ask for you." Ten minutes later, she came back with some cold margarine-smeared toast. Barry nibbled it, worried at how little he could taste, how unsteady his hands were.

More time passed. He didn't feel like reading or watching TV. A couple of the patients had visitors: wives or girlfriends who sat beside their beds, talking quietly. Barry wondered how long he'd be here. Should he phone one or two friends to let them know where he was? There didn't seem much point until he'd spoken to the doctor. For that matter, where exactly was he? He meant to stop someone passing by and ask them, but the fading light made him lose focus and he dozed uneasily for a while. Thinking about the office, the union. If he'd kept in touch with those people, maybe he'd have more friends now.

The nurse woke him up, taking his pulse and injecting the medication into his left arm. There was a bruise there from the last injection, but he didn't feel any pain. "How's it going?" she said.

"Not so bad. Tired."

"You need to rest. I forgot the doctor's on a training course today. We're going tomorrow, so there'll be agency nurses here—and over the night shift. You'll see the doctor in the morning."

"Who was the old man who came round and looked at everyone? He didn't say anything. Was he the doctor?"

The nurse looked uncomfortable. "No, he's the head of the finance company that's running the hospital now. He's going to lead the training course in market awareness." Her voice was hardly above a murmur. She glanced at her watch again. "Well, Barry, I must get on. Take care." She straightened the blanket over him, then walked away. He realised he'd forgotten to ask her which hospital this was. No point in calling her back.

Later, his eyes opened and he realised he'd been asleep. The blinds were drawn, and the lights were dimmed. He needed the toilet, but when his feet touched the dusty floor he lost confidence and settled for using a cardboard bottle. Luckily, the toast hadn't worked its way through his system yet. From somewhere in the ward, he could hear the monotonous voice of a TV newscaster.

What was he going to do when he left hospital? Strangely, that question seemed easier to answer now than before. Get well, get more sleep, find work. The fears he'd been carrying for months seemed unreal, black water passing under a bridge. Now he had an opportunity to make connections.

The night shift—the agency nurses—were moving from bed to bed, making notes and setting up equipment. Their uniforms were the dark, unreal blue of a night sky. One of them, a young man, took Barry's left hand and felt his pulse, then jabbed a needle into the vein of his wrist. Without speaking, he attached the syringe to a drip stand holding a bag of crimson fluid.

"Do I need a transfusion?" Barry asked.

The nurse looked at his face for the first time. "Why are you trying to resist change?"

"Do you even know my blood group?" The nurse seemed to find the question not worthy of an answer. Barry tried another tack: "I was only admitted today. Can you tell me what hospital this is?"

The nurse shrugged. "It's not about where you are," he said. "It's about where you're going." He marked something on a clipboard, attached it to the foot of the bed and walked on.

Hours passed. Barry felt too tired to do anything, but he couldn't sleep. The ward seemed colder than before. The ache in his chest was building again. Had the agency nurse forgotten to give him his medication on time? He looked up and down the ward, but couldn't make out any blue uniforms. Then he saw a figure coming through the doorway, walking very slowly. It was the old man. He took something from the front pocket of his jacket, then leaned over and put his hand on one of the patients. With some difficulty, he straightened up, then crossed over to another bed and repeated the process.

When the visitor reached the bed next to Barry's, he paused again. Barry turned his head very slightly to see what was happening. For some reason he didn't want to attract the old man's attention. The patient in the bed hadn't moved in a while; he was lying face up. As the hospital executive looked down at the patient, Barry noticed how faded his suit was: though made of good material, it was nearly worn through at the knees and elbows. He was completely bald, and he had no eyebrows. His wrinkled hand reached once more into his jacket pocket, brought out a slender wad of banknotes. Carefully, the old man spread the notes in a fan on the chest of the unconscious patient.

Barry couldn't breathe until the executive had passed by. He felt shaky and weak. The faulty strip light must have blacked out. He looked at the banknotes on the sleeping patient's chest. They didn't stir. Between the beds, the hanging bag of blood glistened faintly. A pale air bubble was moving slowly up the plastic tube towards the bag. Moving upwards due to gravity, of course: the blood was moving down. Then Barry saw a second tube coming out of the bag, leading down behind the drip stand. Another air bubble was moving down that tube, towards the floor.

He tried to loosen the syringe fastened to his wrist, but there was no feeling in either hand. His vision was blurred. Dark spots floated across the ward, like air bubbles in reverse. Dust was thick under the strip lights. The visitor was no longer within sight. The invisible hand that pressed down on his chest, forcing the breath out of him, was too strong to be that of an old man. It must have got colder in the ward, because he could see his own breath turning white above his face.

There was no light. Barry was moving through a corridor, somewhere beneath the ground level of the hospital. From ward to ward, office to office, he'd tried to find the old man. In one room he'd seen bodies stacked on shelves from floor to ceiling, brought in on stretchers by blue-clad nurses clearing beds to make way for new patients. In another room he'd seen plastic tubes snaking down the walls towards a long, shallow trough filled with blood. And there had been wards full of the dead and the dying. A concerto of silence.

Finally, a long way down, he could hear echoes of a monotonous voice. He followed them to the lit windows of a lecture theatre. Inside, over a hundred people were sitting and looking up at a stage. The audience were men and women in nurses' uniforms—some grey, some blue. On the stage was a bald man in a new charcoal-grey suit of the best quality. He had no eyebrows. His skin was gleaming with health, and his smooth hands were gesticulating as he spoke.

Barry couldn't make out the words, but he could hear the ripples of applause that followed each statement. And with it, another sound: a faint groan, a whispered lament, no louder than the wind blowing through leaves. It was coming from behind him. All around the theatre, he could see the bloodless faces of the dead. They were pressed together like torn sheets of paper, crammed against the windows, unable to get through or be heard. At that moment, he realised it didn't matter how many of you there were. Without a voice, you were lost.

Bitter Angel

Hello, Michael. It's good to see you again. I've missed you. Can you hear me? I don't know if you recognise me, even. It's Lee. Do you remember? The nurse wouldn't tell me whether you can understand things. The last time I came here, you were covered in bandages. Now I can see it's you. But what's damaged or lost inside, nobody seems to know. I just—I want to tell you that I think I understand what happened to you and Jason. I've made sense of it.

And I want to tell you that I love you. As a friend I mean. We've been friends for nine years. I guess we were more than that for a couple of nights. But they were a long time ago, and months apart. It's friendship that lasts for me. For you, I know it was different. I've never felt about anyone the way you did about Jason. The way you still do, I suppose. That's why you can't come back. But you've made it this far, so maybe you can go further. Anything's possible.

Cleveland Tower is a ruin, by the way. Half the city centre burned down that night in August. People are coming back, but the anger's still there. The army won, of course. The papers say all that matters is restoring stability. But that means preventing change. And the government was all for making people accept change when it came from above. You said that to me last summer, do you remember? In one of your midnight e-mails. Before it all fell apart.

I remember when you first told me about Jason. He'd come down from Blackburn when his company relocated. I think you met at the Pride weekend, roaming the streets at two in the morning. You called him the Angel of the North, after that sculpture you went to see a few years ago. Jason was your type, I guess: small, dark-haired, intense. I met the two of you in New Street that summer; it was obvious you were mad about each other. All the time it was like you were dancing together and the music had just stopped for a moment. When you were alone together it would start again.

You used to e-mail me on nights when he wasn't with you. One time you told me about a dream you'd had. A boy with wings, flying into the sunset, above the city's black skyline. Then the wings catching fire. And you thought he'd flown too close to the sun, until you noticed the sniper on the ground.

Another time, I think you'd been drinking, you told me you'd never really known what making love could be like until you met Jason. The sleepless nights when you just couldn't leave each other alone. You'd stock the fridge with cold food and fruit juice, so you could stay in bed all weekend. And how there were—as you put it—no limits, no barriers between you, physical or emotional. Lucky old you, was my reaction. Actually that wasn't all of my reaction.

Then you told me Jason had lost his job and moved in with you. So the two of you had a bird's-eye view of the city, from the eighteenth floor, when the riots and protests started. You said that where the view had been a fixed pattern of lights like a constellation, now it had swirls of flame like a comet. The trouble only happened in the major cities, so I was safe from it out in Hagley. I did think about coming into Birmingham to join the protesters, but

I didn't have the guts, and then it was too late. Once the army had moved in and closed the roads.

You sent me an e-mail describing the two of you standing naked on your balcony in the early hours of the morning. You'd been making love, but neither of you could sleep. Jason was behind you, his arms twined with yours, and you thought about flying together. From the streets below, you could just hear the sirens. By then, the army had imposed a curfew. Jason kissed you, and you thought his skin was too warm, maybe he had a fever. His left hand was bandaged from where he'd fallen on the steps outside the tower, slipped on broken glass and landed on more of it. Nobody was cleaning the streets any more.

The next night, you told me Jason was very sick. You'd gone out in the day to try and find a doctor or a pharmacy, but the roads were closed off and the soldiers wouldn't help you. He needed antibiotics, you said. His hand wasn't too bad, but the infection had got into his bloodstream. All you had was painkillers and bottled water. Then you e-mailed me at six in the morning to say you hadn't slept all night. Jason was unconscious on a bed soaked with sweat. There'd been more fires and shooting in the city.

It was a Sunday. I e-mailed you twice that morning, but didn't hear back until late afternoon. All you said was: *Jason has been dead for a few hours. At least he was unconscious when he died. Do you feel pain in your sleep? He looks peaceful now. I want to bury him, but there's nowhere to go. The fires are closing in all around. When I open the window I can smell smoke, taste ashes on the wind. I keep asking him what I should do. Maybe if I hold him close, he'll find a way of telling me.*

I read that three times, trying to work out what I could say to you that might possibly help. Then when I tried to click on "Reply", the screen froze. That was when they shut down the broadband, there was no internet access for two days. I don't really know what happened in Birmingham—or London, or Manchester, or a few other cities—in between. All the violence was blamed on rioters and looters. But there were thousands of deaths: tower blocks burned down, people shot in the road, burned in their cars or their homes. I lost a lot of friends that weekend.

If I hadn't seen the newspaper story, I would have gone on thinking you were dead. I suppose at that time, a survivor was more newsworthy than a fatality. It was a short item in the local paper, with the headline "Insane suicide leap fails". Two young men had been found lying together on the pavement, one dead and one alive. The survivor was underneath with the dead man tied to his back. Their arms were bound together with strips of cloth. According to a pathologist, both men had fallen from a dangerous height—but the dead man had actually died several hours before the fall. The other man must have intended to kill himself by leaping. He was still in a coma. Both men had been identified. They gave your names.

There was still a curfew, but the restored internet access and phone lines enabled me to track you down to the City Hospital. Identifying myself as a long-time friend of yours, I talked to the ward matron and a policeman who said you might be charged with mistreatment of a dead body, if you were fit to stand trial. You'd opened your eyes, but they were unable to get any reaction from you. That was a week ago. Maybe you'll come back if you think there's something to come back for. I don't have any answers for you, except that having made it this far is not something you should waste. Love is powerful no matter how much grief it causes.

You see, the police and the nurses assume you jumped off the roof of a house by the university, or maybe out of a low-flying helicopter. But I know you jumped out of Cleveland Tower in the city centre. You and Jason fell nineteen floors—and three miles to the south. Together you got beyond range of the fire. But of course, in the end you had to come back down.

After the Fire

Theresa and I were friends at Birmingham University. We were in the same film and literary societies. We were going through the same kind of delayed adolescence: after years of protective family life and obsessive studying, the adult world was hitting us with the force of a revelation. I wrote poems about it; Theresa lived it. She was a thin-faced, rather sardonic girl who moved as if she was underwater. Her dark, tangled hair completed the illusion.

Over the three years of studying we spent a lot of time together. Theresa wanted me as a male best friend, someone who loved her but wouldn't try to be her boyfriend. Someone she wouldn't have to fall out with. I accepted that role, but never stopped being jealous of the boys who shared her narrow bed. There were times when I would have happily exchanged being her confidant and guardian for an hour in her arms. Even if it meant I was history the next morning. History is a good thing to be sometimes.

My happiest memories of Theresa are from those years. Walking with her down the long avenues of the university campus, past the old red-brick buildings and the clock tower, putting the world to rights. Drinking real coffee in her room, a subtly ordered nest of film posters, wood carvings, second-hand books and CDs. Arguing about the merits of Polanski, Tindersticks, or Militant. Watching foreign films, then finding a quiet table where we could relive the key moments.

We kept in touch after graduating, and somehow both stayed in the city. I studied for a doctorate, while Theresa became a journalist. We used to go and see local bands in Moseley, a suburb with a lot of student accommodation and live music. Both of those features would change before long. In the nineties, Moseley had about it a kind of bohemian aura: a mystical energy with little to sustain it except drugs, alcohol, and a music that was painfully retro even then. I fed on that as a writer; Theresa fed on it as a person. Some things never change.

Theresa was maybe eighteen months out of university when she met the love of her life. Mark looked rather like her but was thinner, almost gaunt. There was something of the gypsy or Middle European about him. When they started going out together, I heard a rumour or two to the effect that he was a jealous lover—and maybe not beyond knocking a woman around. I decided not to say anything about that to Theresa. She could look after herself. Maybe jealousy was still eating away at me, somewhere in the depths that I was so good at mining but couldn't really face, then or now.

When I saw them together, Theresa was rather subdued. Mark gave the impression of being somewhere else in his mind, waiting for her to join him. About a month into the relationship, I met her for lunch. She was nervous, alternating between playful excitement and a worrying silence. "He's wonderful," she said. "Never felt so . . . alive. Enjoyed . . . you know. For hours at a time. But sometimes I don't know. If his world and mine are . . . combinable. Maybe I don't want my world." She hardly ate anything. I noticed a bruise on her neck that could have been a love-bite. Her lips were dry and cracking—but then, it was winter.

Not long after that, I spoke to my friend Jason about a party Theresa and Mark had gone to in Acocks Green. I'd missed it. "Theresa wasn't her usual self," he said. "She would have been. But that new man of hers wouldn't let her be with her friends. He kept muttering in her ear, dragging her off to the kitchen. Later, when people were dancing, he pushed her against the wall and started touching her up. It was quite embarrassing."

People are annoying when they fall in love. Whatever they were before changes into half of some deformed couple-thing with its own bad habits and false memories. It's never felt right to me, though I admit my emotional diet consists mostly of sour grapes. I just assumed the old Theresa would come back when she either got used to Mark or got rid of him. Maybe he'd turn out to be all right. It wasn't until I got the letter that I really started to worry.

The letter—Theresa had never been one for e-mails—had no address on it, but was postmarked Kidderminster. The paper was thick and apparently old. There was a faint stain in the top right-hand corner, as if a drink had been knocked over it. Her handwriting, as ever, was small but rather jagged. The biro had pressed deep into the paper, leaving ridges on the other side. It was the first letter she'd sent me since our student days, and as yet it's the last.

Hi Gary,
Hope you're keeping well. Just wanted to let you know
I'm staying with Mark at his house in Blakedown.
Trying to stay clear of the Moseley vortex for a while.
There's only so much bad music you can take. I've never
been in a serious relationship before, it's powerful but
scary. You look back at the past and it seems to have
happened to someone else. But I don't want to lose
touch with my friends.

It's quiet here. We go for walks, see films, spend a lot of time in the house. I'm doing some freelance work but looking for a job here. All my stuff is here now, though it took me a while to move, didn't all happen at once.

It's confusing, when things are good with me and Mark I feel better than I'd ever thought was possible, and realise how unhappy I've been in recent years. But then sometimes I feel like he's not there, or I'm not, and I want to get away. I'm caught between his world and mine. Sometimes I just feel lost.

Mark is very intense. He doesn't like me to be with other people. I tell him he's with me whatever I do, but he doesn't believe it. If he knew I was writing to you he'd be angry. I'll tell you what it's like. Like look-ing through a window at a view that's brilliantly lit up half the time and then dark and overcast at other times. Sometimes he behaves as if I really don't matter, but then if I start to pull away he tells me I've got nothing to go back to.

The house is strange. He bought it from his parents, who came from somewhere in central Europe and have gone back there. He says he'll take me there some day; it's a country that doesn't exist any more. Wish he wasn't so secretive. There are old pictures on the walls, black and white sketches, faded scenes from a city more or less in ruins. And religious images—Mark's a believer but he's not trying to convert me, maybe he doesn't think I'm worth it. Some of the house is really comfortable in an old-fashioned way, but some of it's grimy and bare, like he's living in a flat whose rooms are scattered around the house.

In a way, I think the house is a kind of departure lounge for where he wants to take me. That's why he's brought me here. Why it doesn't feel like one thing or the other. Why I feel lost. I'm in love with Mark but nothing else seems real. And I'm not well a lot of the time, feel like I'm sleepwalking. Thirsty, tired. I had a check-up and it's not glandular fever or diabetes. Might be an allergy to something in the house. I told Mark I might be allergic to him. He got really angry.

Gary, I hope you're keeping well. Don't want us to lose touch. I might need your help if things get worse here. I might need a bridge back to my old life.

Miss you,

Theresa xxx

Why had she written to me? There was no return address, so she didn't want me to write back. Perhaps she just wanted me to know how things were with her, in case she did need my help. But that was an oddly selfish, even manipulative way for her to behave. And if Theresa was truly in love for the first time, then her letter made me glad that I wasn't. But then, Mark was obviously a difficult person. I'd got close to a few disturbed people, women and men, and something had always made me back off. I wanted my own life.

A couple of months passed, and I heard nothing further. The winter turned into a restless, uneasy spring. I ran into Ghika in Moseley. She'd worked with Theresa for a year or so at the *Birmingham Mail* office. I asked if they were still in touch. Ghika shook her head. "By the time she left, to be honest, we weren't getting on so well." She told me that a couple of months before quitting, Theresa had seemed to change. "Maybe something to do with her new boyfriend, though she didn't talk about him much. She kept coming into work late, then going off to eat her breakfast, then just not focusing on anything. And she went from being a really good union activist to just using the union to cover for not doing any work.

"When her manager told her off for leaving urgent work undone and then lying about it, she took it to the union, said it was victimisation. I was the MoC then. I talked to various people. It was obvious she was in the wrong. I told her so. She quit the union. A couple of weeks later, she quit the job to go freelance. I hope she can sort herself out. I did really like her at first." I didn't know what to say. It was the first I'd heard of the whole episode.

On the Saturday before Easter, I was woken by the phone ringing. "Gary?" It was Theresa. Her voice sounded torn, as if she had a sore throat. "I need to get away from him. Can't go on like this. Can I stay with you?"

"Yes, of course." The flat was in no state for guests, but I could attempt an emergency tidy. "What's happened?"

"Can't talk now." Her voice dropped to a murmur. "I'll be at yours by this evening. About six o'clock. Thanks . . ." She rang off.

I spent a few hours cleaning and tidying the flat and making up a spare bed on the sofa, then went out to buy some food. By late afternoon it looked slightly less like the home of a serial killer. The phone rang a few times, but it wasn't her. When she still hadn't come at eight o'clock, I prepared and ate a quick supper. Not sure what I was supposed to do. I didn't even know where she was, and suspected she didn't either.

Just before eleven, Theresa phoned. "Gary, I'm sorry." Her voice was very quiet. "He drove to Kidderminster Station, stopped me before I got on the train. He didn't force me to come back. Just looked at me." She was breathing hard. "It's better this way. You wouldn't want me around. No-one would." Before I could say anything, she rang off once more.

I kept the sofa bed made up for another fortnight, in case she changed her mind. Then I just tried not to think about her. Even in the Internet age, people could disappear if they wanted to. As the spring rains dried up and what would be a fiercely hot summer began, I received a postcard with a photo of Heathrow Airport. On the back were the words: *Gary—flying out tonight. T xx*

Out of the blue, Theresa phoned me one night in October. "I'm at Birmingham Airport," she said. "Came back on my own. I need someone to talk to." An hour later, she knocked at the door of my flat. She was carrying a travelbag and wearing a heavy black coat I hadn't seen before. I was shocked at how tired she looked. Her black eye makeup couldn't disguise the shadows. It was raining; when she shook the water droplets from her hair, I noticed she was turning grey.

I made some coffee. She asked for a glass of water and drank it in a single gulp. "How are you?" she asked. "Anyone new in your life?" There was, I told her, but it wasn't serious. "I'll never be serious about someone again," she said. The coffee revived her a little, but behind the fatigue was a raw fear that I'd never seen in her before. It made her face like a mask.

"He took me to some town in Hungary," she said. "We were looking for his parents, but they'd moved on. We kept going from place to place, staying in hostels, sleeping in railway stations a few times. I wasn't well, but Mark said we couldn't afford a doctor. He told me his real name once. I don't remember it." She wiped her eyes. "Those little towns, they were all falling apart. No money, no work. But it wasn't just that. I mean, what I was seeing, it was Mark's world. Dust and ashes, dead leaves, rotting stone." She shivered violently. "He said I was learning to see the reality under the skin of life."

"Have you seen a doctor since you came back?" I said. "Sounds like you haven't been well at all."

"I will soon. We were under a railway bridge. He was sleeping, and I just got up and walked up the steps to the bridge. I was going to jump off. But then I saw a station not far away. I had just enough money for the train. Got a flight home. Don't ask me how I paid for it. I had to get away."

"Will he come back, do you think?"

"I'm sure he will. But he won't have me again." Theresa reached out and gripped my hand. "Thanks for being here."

"I just want you to be safe. Have you got a place to stay?"

She shook her head. The skin was tight over her cheekbones. "I gave up the flat. All my stuff's in a lock-in."

"You're welcome to stay here," I said. "Is there anything you need? Something to eat maybe?"

"Just some water," she said. "Thanks."

I made up a bed on the sofa, as before. When I looked back at the table, Theresa had lowered her head into her hands; her eyes were closed. "Looks like you really need some sleep," I said. "We can talk in the morning." It was nearly midnight in any case, and I had work the next day.

Some time during the night, I felt a hand on my shoulder. "Gary." In the light coming through the doorway, I could see Theresa's silhouette. "Can't sleep. I'm frightened. Please hold me." I sat up and put my arms around her. The tension in her thin body was like static electricity. She pressed her face against mine and we kissed. Her breath was sour, but that didn't stop me.

We got under the covers and made love. It wasn't easy, but it was Theresa and that made it important, at least for me. What or who she was thinking about, I don't know. But afterwards, the tension seemed to leave her. She turned away, and I heard her breath slow into the rhythm of sleep.

All I could think of was kissing her taut face as she pressed against me, her eyelids wet from tears.

The alarm clock woke us both abruptly. Theresa looked shattered, but she managed to smile. "Thanks for helping me sleep," she said. I switched on the bedside lamp as she sat up, and was disturbed by how much she'd aged. Maybe I don't look great in the mornings either. When she slipped out of bed I noticed a dark birthmark on her side, like a map of an unknown country.

By the time I needed to leave for work, Theresa had made up skilfully; only her movements gave away how tired she was. She'd drunk some coffee, but hadn't wanted any breakfast. "What are you going to do?" I asked.

"Go to social security and the YWCA," she said. "I can get some freelance work while I'm looking for a job."

"You should see a doctor," I said. "You can't do much if you're ill."

"Now I've left *him* I'll be all right." She gripped my hand. "Thanks, Gary. Now I have to sort myself out. I'll call you in a day or two."

We kissed goodbye in the street. I didn't see her or hear from her for another three years.

It was the spring of 1998. I was in the city centre at lunchtime. Around me, bank employees were walking stiff-backed along the pavement, phones pressed hard to their ears. The government had just announced that from now on, students would have to pay their own tuition fees. That meant that to have access to university education, people like me and Theresa would have to spend a decade crippled by debt. The rights we'd taken for granted were gone forever. I wondered if Theresa was still alive. Why had she really gone to bed with me? I didn't believe it was just for the sake of a few hours' sleep. Maybe she'd known that she'd never come back. My eyes were blurring; I rubbed them, then saw Theresa waiting at the number 50 bus stop.

It couldn't be her. The woman had the rigid posture of someone much older, and her hair was entirely grey. But as I passed, she looked at me and smiled. "Gary. My God, it's you."

I reached out an arm, expecting her to fade like mist, to leave my hand chilled and numb. But she was real, and her lips on my cheek were warm. "I tried to call you," she said. "But you'd moved. Where you used to live, it's all boarded up now. I've been back here for two months. Moved into a new flat."

Her bus arrived; while it was releasing passengers, Theresa wrote her number on a scrap of paper. "Got to go. Phone me. Come round."

The next evening, I went to visit her. The flat was part of an old house on the Alcester Road, not far from where she'd lived before. It had small leaded panes at the tops of the windows. Theresa opened the door and smiled as if to say *You again*. She hugged me and gestured to a chair. "Lovely to see you," she said. "I thought you'd left the area."

"You're back to stay?" I asked.

"Think so. He came back for me, you know. Took me to Blakedown, then to Hungary again. It was worse the second time. He said it was me, the pollution of my body and mind, destroying the landscape. I got away again, but he stayed in my head. Got so bad I was in hospital for a month. I'm still on medication, but I'm all right. It's good to be back here. To see Moseley again. See you again. It's good to have my things around me. They've been in a lock-up for years. Makes me feel like Theresa again."

She glanced around the room, then looked back at me and smiled. I couldn't speak. Wherever I looked in the room—the shelves, the cabinet, even the table—there was nothing but hundreds of empty, dust-covered bottles.

The Anniversary of Never

On a bright April morning, Matt overslept and had to get ready in a rush. By skipping coffee he managed to eat breakfast, shower, and get dressed within half an hour. Something from his restless night was bothering him, maybe some fragment of a dream he'd forgotten. But the train would take him away from that. Hastily buttoning his shirt, he pulled back the bedroom curtains. At least there was no rain. He turned towards the door—but then, despite the time, turned back. What was wrong with the garden?

It took him a few seconds to recognise what had changed. On the small cherry tree by the left-hand fence, the leaves had turned black. It wasn't smoke: the fence and the long grass were unmarked. But the new leaves were prematurely dead, hanging from the twigs like ashes from a bonfire or the tatters of a burnt cloth. He'd have to look at it more closely after work.

In spite of the sunlight, it was a cold morning. The ticket office was closed, a black screen covering its window. The train was so packed that some people couldn't get on, and you had to stand dead still to avoid touching other passengers more closely than was appropriate before the third date. Matt bought his ticket at the station, then ran up the long road to the office where he worked. He couldn't shake off a sense of darkness waiting behind the sky. A memory was nagging at him, something to do with an orchard in winter. But where or when, he had no idea. Probably just as well. He arrived at the office barely in time. The general manager had a thing about timekeeping, and keeping up appearances generally—perhaps because the company, like most around here, was steadily going out of business.

At lunchtime, Matt realised he'd forgotten to make any sandwiches. He walked out to the shop, passing the windowless black wall of a new strip club. Sunlight glittered from a broken bottle on the pavement, and the smell of cider brought back the memory. Evesham, it must have been, a family trip. Walking across fields, they'd passed a derelict farmhouse and reached an orchard. Its trees were bare, huddled in on themselves. Tiny apples, blackened by frost, were scattered on the hard ground. Their odour, a blend of alcohol and decay, had made him giddy. There was no colour in the landscape. He'd picked up an apple and felt its soft, wrinkled tissue on his palm, slightly warm to the touch.

The shop was one of the new mini-supermarkets that were taking over the city centre. Only major chains could afford the rents. He paid at a self-service till and took a plastic-wrapped pasta back to the office. At those prices, he'd better not forget his lunch again. And the image of a rotting apple had spoiled his appetite. Though he knew the memory was too clear to be real. Above the dark office buildings, gulls were circling. What were they looking for? Matt shivered. It felt like winter had come back.

That evening, he noticed the calendar in his kitchen— a series of woodland images—was still on March. He turned over the page, but there was a printing fault: the April photo was just a black square, with no dates under it. Matt tried to cook some food, but his hands were shaking too badly. He needed to talk to someone. Maybe his friend, Alice, in Leicester—she'd known him before things had started to go wrong. Where was his address book? After an hour of searching for it, he gave up and went out for a walk. There seemed to be roadworks in every street, trenches revealing the darkness under the pavement.

Another childhood memory woke him in the night. A visit to the seaside, somewhere on the Devon coast. Walking along the cliff path, then down wooden steps to a small bay. Black jellyfish drying like blood clots on the sand. The sea itself black with oil, its surface perfectly still. His parents walking ahead of him, silent. Matt woke struggling for breath. The alarm clock was the only light in the room. That wasn't a real memory, he was sure. Because he knew where the real ones had gone.

The next day was almost normal. Only the newsagent by the train station, a gap in his front teeth that hadn't been there last week. But that could be real, the shop was open late and things were terrible these days. Though you wouldn't know it from the newspapers he sold. At work, the general manager called a staff meeting to tell them a restructuring of the company was about to happen. "You need to change your mindset," she said. "It's no good saying we should do anything because that's how we used to do it. Change is the norm." Matt glanced at her eyes: they were dull black holes. But that was nothing new.

At the end of the day, he made a phone call. *Six o'clock,* the voice said. *Don't be late. I want to get home.* He ran through the chaos of Snow Hill, the streets crammed with traffic, the old buildings derelict or being torn down. Tall new buildings, hotels and banks, reflected fragments of the sunset. Car exhaust fumes turned white in the air, like breath. Beggars, some of them young, waited in doorways and at pedestrian crossings. Gulls swooped through the gaps where shops and pubs had been. Matt wondered what he was hoping to achieve. He had no more money to offer. At least the old man had agreed to see him.

But the office was no longer there. He recognised the building, but a sheet of rain-blackened wood covered its doorway. On the first floor, where the old man had conducted his business, a few pieces of broken glass clung to the window-frames. There was no notice of relocation. Not for the first time, Matt wished he'd kept his mobile. Spam calls had prompted him to drop it in the rubbish bin. But he knew the real reason: it had been a constant reminder of why he'd bought it, those calls to the police and the hospital. When the world had fallen away and he'd seen what was beneath it. In the end, what could you do?

The call-box on the street corner reeked of stale urine. Matt reached in his pocket for the old man's card and stabbed out the digits. The phone rang for a long time before the voice said, "Hello?"

"Hello, it's Mr. Johnson. I went to your office but you'd moved. The building's empty now."

There was a pause. "I see. You're really in trouble, aren't you?"

"Things are missing all the time. Turning black. And I'm getting memories that are the same. Not real memories. Just things blackened. Burned. But more real than what I *can* remember. Can you help me?"

Another pause. The old man coughed. "This weather's killing me. I'm sorry, Mr. Johnson. There isn't much I can do. What I sold you . . . if there was a way back and I could sell it to you, I'd make you a deal. But there just isn't one." He coughed again. Matt listened to his laboured breath.

Finally the weak voice said: "Once you get into the business of forgetting, you can't cherry-pick what to lose and what to hold onto. The only way is to start again. Buy yourself a new address book. And remember . . . " His voice dissolved into a series of painful coughs. Matt waited for him to finish the sentence, but there was no more.

"Thank you," he said, and hung up the phone. It was still rush hour, but the side-street was empty. Matt cupped his hands and blew into them, noticing that the little finger of his right hand had turned black. He clenched both hands into fists and slipped them into his coat pockets, then walked on to Snow Hill Station and the evening.

The Messenger

You can't really call where I come from a town. It was a village before the industrial revolution filled it with factories and cut it up with railway lines and canals. Now it's an urban district, but nobody's really sure which of three towns it belongs to. A decade ago, there was a lot of talk about regeneration: replacing the dead factories with new software and electronics workshops, and redesigning the landscape to match. But it didn't take hold of our end. The scars of industry were too deep. There's a new hypermarket, a new expressway, but inside people the old map is still there. And I'd moved away, except not.

The house I grew up in was narrow but deep: front room, stairs, living room, and kitchen in a line, like a journey from the street into our private world. Upstairs was a hallway with the three bedrooms and the bathroom all on the left-hand side: my parents' room, then my brother's, then mine. From my window I could see over our paved back yard to the wasteground that had been a landfill site in the factory years. The ground was uneven: metallic soil and broken stones coating the outlines of mounds and filled-in pits. A few scraggy trees and thorn bushes grew there, and fireweed sprouted white feathery seeds that clung to everything.

Paul, my brother, was a year older than me. He was always a quiet boy—could talk but didn't like to. You had to look at his face to know what he was thinking. There were quite a few kids like that on the estate. When we were small he used to have bad dreams, wake up sweating and crying, and come into my room to talk to me. Looking back I suspect he was having fits, but nobody knew. He dreamt of things living under the wasteground: there were tunnels down there, he said, with rats that were totally blind, giant woodlice and moths that never flew.

In my teens I was busy with boyfriends, didn't bother so much with Paul. He spent a lot of time wandering around the canals and the disused factories, in a world of his own. Then he and two other misfit types at the school started playing music together, they both had guitars and Paul sang. They called themselves Mercury. I saw them rehearsing a few times, they were clumsy but there was something there: a kind of fear and excitement they shared. Paul's voice sounded like there was something vile in his mouth he couldn't spit out.

I was fifteen when Paul disappeared. He'd gone off on his own, the way he usually did, not telling anyone where he was going. We didn't wait up for him, but in the morning when he wasn't there our dad phoned the police. They never found him, and there was no sign of another life— drugs or lovers—that could have claimed him. I think I'd have known if he was seeing someone, but I'm not sure. His two musician friends said they knew nothing. The band didn't carry on.

Six months later, my mother was diagnosed with a brain tumour. She'd been tired for a while, complaining of headaches and everything being too dark, but we'd thought she was just depressed about Paul. Then she blacked out on the stairs, woke up but couldn't move, was taken into the local hospital. She was sent home but went downhill fast. One day I came home from school and my father was standing in the front porch, as if sheltering from the rain, though the sky was clear. I looked at him and he just shook his head.

Two other people in our street had died from cancer in the last year. My aunt Jane, my mother's elder sister, had died of leukaemia when I was a toddler, and the fear of it had been in my mother's voice for years. Now people were talking about a "cancer cluster" on the estate and in our street. The local paper said there'd been forty-seven deaths in ten years, among just a few hundred people. And it mentioned the landfill site, how a chemicals factory had dumped its waste there for forty years before a fire put it out of business.

The council took soil samples, did tests and said there was nothing toxic in the ground—at least, no more than was typical for the region. But a scientist from the local university said there were abnormally high levels of mercury, caesium, and other poison metals. The issue disappeared into the hazy depths of local government. Meanwhile I'd left home and got a job thirty miles away. My father stayed in the house, trying to fill it up with empty bottles. Sometimes the silence of loss stops people talking to each other. It's nothing to be proud of, but it happens.

One weekend, a few months after moving out, I went back for a visit. My father took me out to the pub. I got the feeling he was more at home there than in his narrow house. We traded jokes in local dialect—*I'm afraid them cor be med, yow'll 'ave to buy 'em*—and drank pints of a dark local beer which I'd never liked, but now felt I ought to. When I asked him about the toxic waste investigation, he shook his head. "Nothing down there, Lucy. It was too long ago. Nothing there. People always try and dig up the past, but it's no use to anyone."

As we walked back to the house, I could smell the landfill site in the still night air. Living away had made me less used to it. It was a cold smell like decay held in check: bad meat at the back of the freezer, its bruises covered up by ice crystals. My father got another two beers out of the fridge, but I said I was too tired to stay up. The door to Paul's room was closed; I pushed it open quietly and looked inside. The room was bare. I went to my own room, undressed in the dark, lay down on the familiar bed and tried to sleep.

Three years went by. I worked in advertising, helping local companies to design their brochures and leaflets, did some photography on the side. That was before it went digital, and the mystery of seeing an image harden in the developing fluid took my breath away. I bought lightproof blinds so I could use my bedsit as a dark room. A couple of local magazines published my photos of old factories and railway bridges, but after a while I lost confidence. The thought of what might be hidden behind those crumbling walls kept nagging at me.

Also, I was going to the doctor more and more often. Minor things, the usual aches and nausea from crowded trains and polluted air, made me panic. Sometimes the fear was so intense that I blacked out, then spent the rest of the day in a dazed state with the same few minutes replaying over and over. Then, for no reason, the fear would lift and I'd sense the world full of energy, a secret life coming through in waves, brighter and brighter until I was almost flying above the street, and then the daylight would begin to splinter and I'd close down again, checking myself all through for signs of a hidden pathology.

My long-suffering doctor eventually referred me to a psychologist. I told her about the cancer cluster, my mother's death, Paul's dreams, the photographs, how some days I could see the wasteground more clearly than the buildings around me. She agreed that regular health checks were a good idea, within reason. And I told her how the daylight seemed to brighten and then drain away every few days. She said I had a mercurial temperament. I laughed at that and couldn't explain why, at least not to her.

By then I'd read about Mercury, the messenger who could pass between worlds, from the gods to the humans and back again. He led Orpheus into the underworld to find Eurydice. That was the problem down our end, I thought: we didn't have a messenger or envoi, just a funny accent and a history that had no pull for tourists. She prescribed some pills that took the edge off, though I could sense the same fear reaching for me through the chemical fog.

It was about six months later that the dreams started. I was working long hours and had just become involved with a man who lived some distance away, so we spent more time talking on the phone than actually together. After a long, frustrating call from him, I fell asleep and had the sensation of crawling through darkness, then emerging into some kind of passage where the only light came from faintly glowing figures half-embedded in a wall of packed earth. They were human bodies, motionless, their eyes closed. I could hear them breathing. A kind of pale webbing covered them, fixing them to the soil. I recognised them as friends from school, though no names occurred to me.

The passage divided into two, each lined with still figures. If I carried on walking through the warren of decay, eventually I would find Paul. The terror of that woke me up, struggling for breath. I rushed through the morning ritual of washing and dressing, cleaned my teeth, checked my change for the train, then picked up my watch and saw it was just after three a.m.

The same dream recurred every few nights for a month. I never knew how I'd reached the tunnels or how I might get out again. There seemed to be hundreds of people trapped down there, silent but alive, wrapped in white cobwebs. The air had the cold smell of the landfill site. Somehow I knew that if I saw Paul down there, it would be a sign. There would be a change in me: the aches and the sickness would have a meaning, and then the fear would be nothing more than a photograph of the way it was, the way it always had been.

The night train passed through a landscape of dead and living industry: factories lit up for the night shift beside others whose narrow windows were empty or bricked up. Behind the silhouettes of bridges, lights floated on canals and streets of terraced houses repeated themselves in the distance. Layers of time were closing around me, drawing me home. The train shuddered to a halt.

My father opened the door and embraced me in a distracted way, as if he was expecting someone else. At least his breath didn't smell of alcohol. He took my arm and guided me past various heaps of rubbish to the kitchen, where old newspapers were scattered over the table. I wondered if he'd been carrying out some kind of chemical experiment—but then I realised he'd annotated the papers with a stubby pencil, and the smell was a half-eaten meal abandoned hours or days before. They were local papers from the sixties, before I was born.

"It's all here," he said, "if I can just see what it means. The chemicals factory, why it burned down, what was really going on. I'm asking round the pub for people's old papers, stuff they've kept in their garages or garden sheds. Soon I'll work it out. There's just a few more facts I need. What they left out of the books." He gestured to the kitchen shelf, where my mother's cookery books had been replaced with a dozen or more volumes of local history. His eyes were bruised from lack of sleep. "I'll find the answer, Lucy, if it takes me the rest of my life."

I looked in the fridge. There was some cheese and bread that didn't seem too stale, so I made him a sandwich and persuaded him to eat it. Then he fell asleep with his head in his arms, his hands touching the brittle newspapers as if still searching for hidden details. I unbolted the back door, crossed the yard and walked out onto the overgrown surface of the old landfill site. It was a clear April night, and the moon was three-quarters full. Distant streetlamps and passing cars ringed the dark ground with a wreath of faint light.

For two or three hours, I walked back and forth across the uneven patch of land. The old factory buildings on the far side were bricked and boarded up. The troughs and ridges in the ground were hardly visible by moonlight, and I fell any number of times, but I was determined to find the way through. The fear reached me out there, shook me hard, and twice I curled up in the grass and cried until I had no breath or tears left. It was cold out there. Finally I said goodbye to Paul and headed back towards the house.

Just as I reached the paved yard, a flicker of movement caught my eye and I turned back. A stray dog was climbing one of the earth-covered mounds near the edge of the landfill site. It was painfully thin, and its left forelimb was damaged. I watched it struggle to reach the top. Just before it jumped or fell down the other side, out of sight, it turned its narrow head to look at me. The whole of its face was covered with a pale mesh of cobwebs. It made no sound.

My father had gone to bed; the house was dark. I walked up the creaking steps to my room, and lay down on the bed without undressing. Though I'd never believed in any God, I thought then that if I prayed, he might exist and give me a life without visions.

For Christina Morris

For Crying Out Loud

It wasn't exactly a lovers' lane, but then they weren't exactly a couple. Just two young office workers on a date in early summer. They'd been for a drink at the Kerryman in Digbeth and listened to a local singer. That and the warm evening had put them in a tender mood. Ian drove randomly around the backstreets, looking for a quiet place to park, as night fell. Lisa watched the sunset burn through the gaps between workshops and scrap yards. Eventually they stopped under a railway bridge. The car engine shuddered and fell silent. He ran a hand slowly through her auburn hair. They kissed slowly, dusk blurring their faces. Then she froze.

"Can you hear that?" she asked.

Ian shook his head and lowered his mouth to hers. Lisa didn't move. Tears were glittering on her cheeks. "Oh, my God," she whispered.

He touched her arm and felt a shudder pass through her, as if a train had gone by overhead. "Don't," she said.

Though he drew back, she carried on repeating the word and only stopped when he took hold of her and pulled her against him. Lisa was crying so hard she couldn't breathe. Then she looked up at him, a blind darkness in her eyes. "Drive on," she said.

A minute later, he stopped in a narrow street, next to a mound of stripped cars. Evening was draining the colour from the buildings. "What was the matter?"

"Just a voice. I don't know." Lisa's eyes were closed. "Like someone being choked to death. But if you didn't hear it, then . . . " Her hand reached up in front of her face. He slipped his fingers between hers and felt her begin to shake again. It worried him, how cold her hand was. The streetlamps had come on. In one of the factories nearby, a machine snarled into life.

Suddenly Mike felt lost. Towards the city centre, the Grand Union Canal seemed to fall apart. The line of factories ended in a cluster of derelict buildings with no clear identity, the canal surface was broken up with rubbish, and even the bridges were less well made. Clouds of midges shivered above the dull water. It was like a kind of still estuary. He couldn't remember how you got back to street level. At least these ruins were more comforting than the recently boarded-up shops on the Coventry Road.

The sound of traffic was getting louder. Above the next bridge, the sunlight flared from the windows of a new office block. There it was: the worn staircase leading up to Fazeley Street. He was tempted to stay on the canal towpath until trees and silence came back on the far side, but there wasn't time and he was afraid of getting lost. As he neared the steps, a cloud shifted: the sunlight was reflected from the canal, the nearby buildings, like the district was on fire.

That was when he heard the cry. It made him stop, turn around. Where was it coming from? It was so close the voice could have been his own, but with another few steps it faded. He walked slowly back down the stone stairs. There it was again—but how could it go on like that? How could anything scream that way and not die? Mike stood there, looking around, as the cry tore through him. Was it a child? An animal? Nothing was moving, but he could feel a tremor in the ground like the beating of wings.

And then he was running up the stairs, out onto the roadway, a car swerving to avoid him, its horn breaking his trance. The pavement glowed with sunlight, but he was so cold he had to cup his hands around his mouth and blow into them. He walked hastily onward, not daring to stop in case another voice touched him. It took him a long time to reach Digbeth High Street and the bus stop. The sight of St Martin's, the one old building in a cradle of redevelopment, calmed him down. *The long way round*, he thought. Where did that come from? On the bus he remembered: a moment from his childhood. At the back of the Bull Ring market, an old couple laden with shopping, the woman saying, *"We seem to be going the long way round,"* the man replying, *"For cryin' out loud, woman, shut yer face. I know it's the longest bleedin' way of soddin' round, don' I?"*

Lisa had walked from Tyseley to the Swan Centre, though there seemed to be less of it every time she went and the new Tesco hadn't opened yet. Unwilling to use the subway even in daylight, she crossed over the Coventry Road on the narrow walkway, trying not to look down at the stream of traffic. On the far side, traffic cones guided her past a long ditch to the pavement. She was only yards from the entrance to the shopping centre when the cry wrapped itself around her head. She stopped, both hands moving in front of her face, then fell to her knees.

There was no clue. No flowers tied to the lamp-post or police notice stuck to the wall. When had it happened? The voice was old, hoarse with despair. Lisa bit her lips. A passer-by shot her a look of disgust. Then she felt a hand touch her shoulder. "Are you okay?"

She turned her head. A young man, rather pale. She nodded and stood up, keen to get away. This was a place she'd walked through before. It had to mean she was going insane.

Then he said: "Did you hear it too?"

They sat in the Old Bill and Bull, drinking cider and trying to talk about the voices. It wasn't easy. Neither of them liked the g-word for a start. Lisa called them *cries*, Mike called them *echoes*. They agreed that it had something to do with death—probably violent death. Neither of them had experienced anything like it until this summer, when it had happened a few times to both of them. Lisa told him about her date in Digbeth. "He never called me again. I don't know if he was scared or just frustrated." They swapped phone numbers and agreed to keep in touch. Afterwards, Mike wasn't sure if it helped that there was someone else. He wasn't good at sharing.

The next weekend, they met in an Irish pub in Highgate. Lisa said she'd been trying to reconstruct the events behind the cries—who had died there and why. She'd looked online but there was nothing by way of local news that could help. Mike said he was more bothered about where the voices came from, the boundary between worlds. Were they just involuntary sounds or did they have a message? Unable to answer any of these questions, they drank Black Bush and listened to the forlorn jukebox. It turned out they had something else in common: a fondness for "Fields of Athenry", which was so popular among Irish Brummies that he'd even heard its chorus dubbed over rapid beats at a Fox Hollies disco night.

"That song, you know what it's about?" Lisa said. "How the English caused the famine by selling all the wheat grown in Ireland, so the farm workers had nothing but potatoes to live on. A blight on one crop meant that thousands died. And the English Government refused to help in case it created a *nation of mendicants.*"

Mike frowned. "I thought it was more about how loneliness is the same whether you're in an open field or on a prison ship." Lisa gave him a look that was half pity and half curiosity. "Folk songs should have mystery," he said, feeling awkward.

"That's all very well, Mike, but some things are real." As if to underline the point, she gripped his hand. The jukebox moved on to "Donegal Danny". He stared into her dark eyes, but didn't try to kiss her. He didn't want her to think he was doing that because he was drunk, or because she was. And somehow the voices held them apart as well as binding them together.

The undertow of loneliness was more powerful than fear, however, and a week later they slept together for the first time. There was a desire in both of them that the events in Lisa's narrow bed couldn't satisfy. "Not everyone's good at everything," she reassured him.

Perhaps this was the start of love, this hunger for something beyond reality. Perhaps it had to do with the voices, another of which pulled him into its cave of pain on the bridge over Moor Street Station. Or perhaps he needed to spend more time online.

Taking advantage of the bright evenings, they went for some local walks in places not too likely to hold echoes of violence. Neither of them wanted that as an element of their dates. They visited the Lickey Hills, the Ackers, the Sandwell Valley. Mike always found Lisa particularly attractive in such surroundings, but they were never intimate out-of-doors. There was always the sense of being witnessed.

It was Lisa who started the group. She said it was important for "listeners" to share experiences and ideas, try to identify a common purpose. Mike was initially against it: "These are mysteries of life and death, it's not a fucking Facebook group." The way she politicised things was starting to get under his skin. But when Lisa told him three local people had got in touch with her online, he couldn't pass up the chance of meeting them. Perhaps the group could achieve some mystical breakthrough that he couldn't imagine on his own.

They met at the Briar Rose pub in town, the kind of place where you could talk about whatever you liked because no-one else was listening. The other three were older than Mike and Lisa. There was Trevor, a former mental patient who'd assumed the cries to be a new symptom. And Jane, a bitter civil servant who thought the voices were a warning of the coming breakdown of society. And Eamonn, a white-haired Irishman who said very little. They all seemed to hear something terrible in the voices, something that drained the energy from them. Mike was depressed by the lack of any collective vision. When Lisa said she hoped the group would serve as a focus for "the listener community", he laughed harshly and knocked back the last of his pint.

Afterwards, Lisa asked him what he'd been laughing at. Too drunk to hold back, he snapped: "Everything's a *community* these days, isn't it? The this community, the that community, every website, every Yahoo group, every bunch of people with a hang-up or a shoe size in common is a community. It's all just a way of disguising the fact that there's no community, not any more." He expected Lisa to argue, but she just quietly said goodnight.

Despite the alcohol, he had trouble getting to sleep. Why hadn't he been more tactful? It was hard to say what you meant when you didn't know. For some reason he thought of the Asian boy who'd been waiting in a bus shelter late at night when he was walking home, a year before. The bus wasn't running due to local roadworks. Mike had told him that and they'd walked into Yardley together. He'd been drunk that night too, keen to get home and sleep. The boy had asked him if he was married, then said "I don't bother with girls." The next day, Mike had realised the point of that comment. It had saddened him, any failed communication saddened him. Eventually he drifted into sleep. His phone rang during the night, but when he woke up it was silent.

Early the next week, they took a day off to visit the Wren's Nest in Dudley—a nature reserve wrapped around the college where Lisa had studied. Mike had never seen a place like it: miles of woodland, mostly ash, on slopes that plunged steeply below the footpaths. Here and there, limestone rock faces showed through the hillsides. This had been one of the most important fossil sites in Victorian times. Wood-framed steps made it possible to climb through the breathtaking curtains of ash, beech, and oak leaves, the giant trees hung with creepers. Along the footpath, twisted charcoal pillars marked where local kids had started fires.

Mike thought he could make out the faint cries of creatures that had died here, hunted by birds of prey. Like the human voices, they didn't sound far away but rather inside his head. He would have asked Lisa if she could hear them, but she kept talking about something that had happened in London that weekend: the police had shot a young black man, then a protest in Tottenham had turned into a riot. "They dragged him out of a cab and blew his head off. They told the press he'd shot at them, but eyewitnesses said he was unarmed." He didn't want to listen, not out here in this vision made real, on this dizzying overgrown slope. This was a place of eternity.

That evening, the bus taking them back to Birmingham terminated at the north-west edge of the city. The driver said there'd been trouble on the streets. They waited for the number 11, which wouldn't have to go through town, but even that seemed to be cancelled. The only pubs in sight had closed early. Stopping to eat in Dudley had been a mistake, real ale or no real ale. They both lived in East Birmingham—too far to walk, and the centre might be dangerous. Mike wondered how things could have changed so fast. He didn't know the number of any cab firm out here. Eventually they found a curry house that was open and asked the waiter for a number. He let them wait in the restaurant. The cab took nearly an hour to come.

They went back to Mike's flat in Yardley. Lisa didn't want to go home alone, even by cab. She listened to the local news on his radio while he hastily tidied the bedroom. When she came to bed, her face was pale. "All hell broke loose tonight," she said. "People have been killed. I don't understand it." She was trembling. They embraced for a while, but didn't try to make love. It was already past midnight and they had work in the morning.

Mike stared at the front page of the *Birmingham Mail*. The face of Tariq Jahan was taut with grief. He'd tried to resuscitate his own son after looters had run him and two of his friends down in Winson Green. They'd been trying to protect local businesses. The next day Tariq had called for peace, for no violence in response to the killings. His haunted face and stumbling voice had reached across the country, and the riots and looting had ended. When he talked about "community", he meant real people in a real place, people who could die.

There'd been violence all over the city that night. Shops were boarded up in the city centre and the local high streets. He wondered how many of them would reopen. The Prime Minister had said the cause of the rioting was benefits. Even Mike could see how stupid that was. But he couldn't see much point in what Lisa was doing now, going to a meeting held by some political group "against austerity". People needed to look inside themselves.

As night fell, he went out for a short walk. The off-licence near the Swan Centre was open late these days. It was cheaper than drinking in pubs. He paused on the bridge over the Grand Union Canal and looked up towards the city centre. The pill-coated bubble of Selfridges was coloured blue after dark. Recently one of the echoes had caught him as he stood here, sung him its lullaby of eternal pain. But tonight the only sound was the traffic in the distance.

Snow was drifting across the roadway like fine particles of ash. Mike's hands felt like knots of wood, despite his gloves. At least winter meant things would stop changing for a while. He'd been walking for hours, stopping at every pub he saw, trying different brands of gin and white rum. One of them was the pub where he and Lisa had first held hands, but he was past caring. At least they were still in touch. But their relationship was like a pub they'd both been banned from: it hadn't burned down, but neither of them could go there.

He remembered the sunlight filtered through a veil of leaves, making highlights in her auburn hair. The end of August. His memory was gentler when he was drunk than when he was sober. That wasn't the only reason for drinking, but it was one.

The next pub was the last on his way home: the tiny Irish one at the top of the Warwick Road. No more pubs for two miles after that—whether that was due to the past Quakers or the present Muslims, he wasn't sure. It occurred to him that Birmingham's original population was still in the background, but the city took its modern identity from exiles—whether they came from Ireland, Jamaica, or Pakistan, they never went back.

He was just in time for last orders. They didn't have Black Bush, but Jameson's was an acceptable substitute. He gulped the drink and ordered another, mentally showing the bank manager his arse. Something in the corner of the pub caught his eye: an old man's face, fringed with white hair. Had they met before? The old man smiled and Mike remembered: it was Eamonn. The Listeners had met one more time after the riots. Nobody had said as much, but they'd all realised that the voices had gone away.

Eamonn reached out a frail hand as Mike approached him. "How are you keeping?" the old man asked.

"Not too bad. Are you well?"

"Can't say I am. But it's okay. Nice to see you."

"Likewise." They sipped their whiskies. The jukebox had faded; it was drinking-up time, though a pub out here wouldn't be as clock-obsessed as the city centre ones.

"Eamonn, did you ever, you know . . . hear one of those voices again, the cries?"

The white head shook slowly.

"Me neither. But why?" Mike realised his voice had risen, though no-one reacted.

The old man drained his glass, his eyes closed. He beckoned Mike to lean over, then said very softly: "I don't know. But I think . . . they called. That was all. They called, and nobody answered."

All Dead Years

When she saw the case notes, Val's first reaction was *At least she's trying to get help.* She was tired of middle-class Londoners seven-sevening about public transport. Here was someone admitting to an irrational fear of the Underground instead of blaming it on terrorism. That meant there might be a chance of treating the phobia. Val noted that the patient had been on Prozac for a year and it wasn't helping. Therapy was the last resort, as usual.

The initial meeting for assessment was hard work. Helen was so withdrawn she barely agreed at first to what was in her case notes. She was a petite woman in her forties, a few years older than Val, and must have been quite pretty before chronic anxiety had taken the life from her face. Fear of the Underground had forced her to give up her job at the British Museum and work from home, writing public information materials on art history. It had mostly shut down her social and personal life as well. A question about current relationships was met only with a rapid shake of the head.

After nearly an hour, Helen began to describe her symptoms: "As soon as I go underground, I start to feel sick. Like I can't breathe. There are dead things in the walls. If I get onto the Tube I can smell the decay, hear the water dripping, I can't stand it. I have to get out before the journey starts."

Val had expected her to talk about fear of terrorism, or fire, or being mugged—but those manifest fears didn't seem to be part of it. The latent content was right at the surface. Which meant the cause would probably be harder to reach. Helen couldn't speak directly about her state of mind: "It's not a fear, it's already there. Waiting for me."

"You mean it's real?" Val said. Helen nodded, biting her lip. "Where do you think the Tube will take you?"

Helen looked down. Very quietly, she said: "When I look at the Underground map, I can see the real map." She wouldn't be drawn on what that meant, and hardly said anything more. But when Val ended the session by saying that she hoped they'd be able to work together and find some answers, a flicker of hope enlivened the older woman's dull face.

That moment stayed with Val when she left the clinic to get some lunch. It was an overcast day in late spring, the sun's heat filtering through a layer of metallic cloud. Old women and mothers with prams picked their way over the uneven pavement. Val sat on a low wall, drinking a bottle of flavoured mineral water. Her eyes trawled the sky for a trace of sunlight.

Over a series of weekly appointments, Val tried to peel off the psychic bandages from whatever wound Helen was covering up. You had to be careful in a case like this: any real progress towards understanding would be experienced by the patient as a threatening loss of control. It had to be balanced with work at the symptom level, using what Val thought of as "acronym therapies" (NLP and the like) to disinfect the bandages.

Not that the first three sessions revealed much. Helen's childhood seemed to have been happy, and she was still on good terms with her parents. As an only child she'd been a little over-protected, and she'd had a few wild years after leaving home—including a phase as the mistress of an older man—before settling down in her current academic lifestyle. The fear had come on rather suddenly, and at first she'd valued her work and social life too much to consider moving away from London. But now the fear had taken so much away from her that, if the therapy didn't work, she thought leaving might be the only option.

It wasn't until the fourth session that Helen mentioned Paris. Val was encouraging her to relive her last panic attack on the London Underground, when she'd blacked out and woken up in the station attendant's office. Her purse and wristwatch had been stolen on the Tube. "I woke up and didn't know where I was. Thought I was back in Paris. I called out for Don, but he wasn't there."

"Who's Don?"

"That prick." Val hadn't heard her swear before. "The older man. We used to go away together for weekends. Or stay at his summer house in Dorset. In the winter, when no-one was around. His wife didn't know he was there. We had a couple of days in Paris once. I thought I was back in the Underground, trying to run away from him."

She looked at the clock on the wall. "Time's nearly up."

"Doesn't matter," Val said. "I think you should tell me about it."

Helen turned and looked straight at her. There was a trapped energy in her face, words looking for a voice. But it was a couple of minutes before she spoke.

"That trip to Paris, in midweek. He kept telling me the only way I could grasp the mystery of love was to submit to it utterly. He was big on mysticism, and I was young and smitten enough to believe it, or persuade myself I could. We spent the first day walking around Montmartre, all those trees and stone staircases, it was like another world. And then . . . well, we didn't get much sleep. So the next day I was in a bit of a daze. He wanted to go to the Catacombes. I wasn't keen, but he came out with some grand statement about how it was the true face of the city. Made me feel I was ignorant if I didn't go.

"There weren't many people down there. Living I mean. It was cold and damp. A mile of tunnels, lined with bones. They had to clear the cemeteries to make way for new bodies. The remains all ended up there. A wall of femurs, a wall of tibias, a wall of skulls. It made me feel sick. But Don was really excited. He said, 'This is the truth of humanity—this is the end and the beginning', and more crap of that nature. There was a side tunnel being repaired, and I let him drag me into it. We climbed over a wooden barrier. There was a smell of disinfectant.

"I didn't think he was really going to do it, but he pushed me against the wall of bones and put his hand up my skirt. I wouldn't let him. There were cheekbones and teeth pressing into my back. I tried to argue, but he gripped my throat. Then I blacked out. When I woke up, he was sprinkling mineral water over my face from a bottle. He said he was sorry, but the way he said it meant he was disappointed in me. I didn't think he did anything to me while I was unconscious, but at the time I wasn't sure. I was bruised already.

"Later, we were on the underground. It was more bare than in London: there were huge stone-walled cavities without tiles or pictures. When I looked at the window I could see rows of skulls reflected in the glass. Don put his hand on my arm. It felt like bone. Suddenly I couldn't breathe. I pulled away and started running, from carriage to carriage, just trying to get away from him, but then I came to the end and stood there until he found me, just as the train came into a station. I'd wet myself. He didn't say anything. Just took my hand and led me off the train.

I think if I'd tried to hold back, he'd have broken my arm."

Helen was crying. Val passed her a tissue. "Did you leave him after that?" she asked.

"Should have done. Instead, I went to stay at his house in Exeter. I'm not ready to talk about that. We were already finished. I shouldn't have gone there. Do you think I'm . . . sick? Do you think I'm a child?"

"You're a human being. Bad times are part of that. I don't much like the sound of this . . . ex-boyfriend of yours. Even now, he's got you blaming yourself for the way he treated you." Val tried to keep her voice level, but she was surprised by the depth of her own anger. Then she glanced at the clock. "Okay, we'd better wind this up. Are you going to be all right, Helen?"

"Don't worry." Her face was very pale, though. Val saw her out, then sat in the reception area for a few minutes before preparing for the next session. The building's air-conditioning was on its last legs, and she imagined she could feel the sun's heat coming through the walls. Her throat was dry. All the phones were ringing. She closed her eyes and thought of rain.

In the following sessions, Helen was reluctant to talk about her last visit to Don's house. "It was miserable," she said in response to Val's prompting. "We couldn't stand each other. He'd turned jealous, like he had any right. And the house was making me ill. It was full of dead things. Why do you want me to talk about it? Some things are best just to forget. My two years with Don—waiting for him, then feeling worse when he was there—those are dead years. Why let him back into my head?"

"What do you mean, the house was full of dead things?"

"Insects. Birds." Helen crossed her arms over her chest. "Can we talk about something else?"

Val made a note to return to the topic later. But no opportunity seemed to arise. Helen wanted to focus on overcoming the fear. She felt it was important for her to travel on the Underground again. Val tried to work with her in the usual way, helping her to identify and challenge her fears.

But at the end of an hour of working carefully through the realities of the Tube network, separating the real dangers from the unreal ones, Helen said: "Just one thing. Not being afraid will enable me to get on the Tube. But how will it help me when the train gets to its real destination?"

Another time, Val talked her through the Paris episode and suggested that her uncertainty about what had happened during her blackout had led to a sense of being contaminated, and hence to feelings of guilt. Helen agreed with that, and seemed much calmer afterwards. But Val wondered if her relief hadn't just come from being offered an answer she could accept.

They met by chance at the Victoria and Albert Museum, which was showing a collection of pre-Raphaelite sketches. Val wouldn't normally have any social contact with a patient—but she felt it would be wrong to brush Helen off when getting out at all was a struggle for her. The older woman had come on the bus, but her fear of subways had made it a slow journey. They were both impressed by the quiet eroticism of the drawings. An entire wall was given over to Rossetti's sketches for his famous Proserpine image. Helen muttered: "Looks like she wishes she'd spat instead of swallowing." Val was surprised to feel herself blush.

In the café, over a pot of Earl Grey tea, they discussed the Tube. Helen had a realistic knowledge of the routes that coexisted with her map of despair. "The Piccadilly line to Green Park, then the Victoria line to Seven Sisters. Less than half an hour. Except I'd never get there."

"I'll come with you if you like," Val said. "Make sure you're safe." Helen shook her head. "Okay, I'll give you my mobile number. Call me when you get to the Tube station."

Helen paused, then nodded. "All right. I'll call in ten minutes." She picked up her embroidered leather hand-bag, gave Val a nervous wave, and left. Val finished her tea. She wasn't sure the signal would reach the café, so she walked outside and sat on a bench. It was a blazing hot day, and the air reeked of traffic fumes and pigeon shit. The trees were wilting, turning yellow ahead of time.

After nearly half an hour, her phone rang. But all she could hear was a faint hollow sound like wind in a tun-nel. A voice was caught up in it, repeating something. Just when she thought the words were becoming clear, the line went dead. Val tried to get the number, but it hadn't reg-istered. She waited a few more minutes, then went home.

Helen called her an hour later. "Sorry, I couldn't face it. Caught the bus."

"I wish you'd let me know," Val said. "I've been worried."

"Sorry. I was embarrassed. I was just trying to make my-self use the Tube. But if I did, you'd never see me again."

"Helen, it doesn't matter whether you use the Tube or not. I'm trying to help you overcome your fear, not put yourself at risk. You should use it when you're ready to, not before."

The older woman laughed softly. "You still don't un-derstand. If I don't go down into the Underground, this summer will last forever."

After that, the sessions seemed to lose momentum. Helen was more relaxed, but her delusions seemed if anything to have hardened into a fatalistic stance. They began to talk about other things—art, films, myths—and Val found herself opening up more, sharing a little of her anger and bewilderment at the tide of ignorance that was sweeping away the ideals she'd once assumed would shape the future. "We're returning to the past and calling that *modernisation*. You wait, the next government will send children to workhouses. Time's running backwards."

Helen's joke about the summer never ending wasn't mentioned again between them, but it was the driest and warmest autumn Val could remember. When had it last rained? The heat was pushing up the violence rate, making her uneasy if she came home late and had to face the Croydon streets after dark. After a series of stomach upsets, she gave up on tap water altogether. Every Tube journey meant running a gauntlet of sweaty bodies and hostile stares. She could smell decay in the tunnels, though that could have been Helen's fear infecting her.

The therapy courses normally lasted a year, but Val decided they'd probably achieved all they could. She'd leave the door open for Helen to contact her in the event of any crisis, and maybe they could keep in touch as friends too. Maybe Helen saw something in her face, because the first thing she said in the next session was: "I need your help. Will you come with me?"

"On the Tube? I said I would."

Helen shook her head. "No, not there. I need you to go back with me. To Don's second home."

Afterwards, Val wasn't sure why she'd said yes. Perhaps there was a greater depth of friendship between them than she'd thought. One of Val's past lovers had been violently jealous, and she respected Helen's struggle to deal with what had clearly been a bad experience. But also, she realised, this might be the only way she could learn the truth.

Nine days later, they caught the train from London Paddington to Exeter. A recent fire had scorched miles of farmland, turning wheatfields into black crusts above which cinders flapped and circled. Though the windows didn't open, Val could smell the reek of charred soil.

They spent most of the journey talking about their university days. It felt strange to remember a time when the future had seemed limitless—though for both of them, the final year had been one of claustrophobic routine. "It's amazing how mature you think you are at that age," Helen said. "But it's all ideas and words, not experience. Being a student is the only time when learning doesn't mark you."

Not far from Exeter, the train went into a tunnel. At once, Helen froze. Her eyes scoured the darkness beyond the window. Val could hear a rustling sound, like rats or birds in a forest, all around them. The sour taste of pollution flooded her mouth. Then the train re-emerged into the afternoon sunlight. Helen's face was dead white, coated with sweat. Silently, Val gripped her hand.

They booked in at a small hotel near the railway station, had a light lunch and walked out to the estuary. The long summer had reduced the Exe to a grey tongue of water in a dry, cracked mouth. "Whenever Don brought me here," Helen said, "I used to think of that line from Swinburne: *Even the weariest river / Winds somewhere safe to sea.* But it doesn't look weary any more. It just looks dead."

Val followed her a couple of miles upriver, then away from the Exe and through a patch of woodland. From a distance, she could see the blackened hulk of a ruined house. A few charred roof-beams were still in place. "It's been like that for twenty years," Helen said. "No-one repairs it or knocks it down. He keeps it the same, to remind me."

Behind the ruined house, the garden was shielded by a ten-foot fence—most of which had withstood the storms of two decades, but a falling tree had ripped through one section. Helen pointed to the gap. She didn't seem in any mood for discussion. The dead tree and the fence-slats seemed to have blended into a rotting floor that it took some effort to negotiate.

The abandoned garden was less overgrown than might have been expected. The long, dry summer had withered the trees and stunted the dense weeds. It was like walking through a faded sepia photograph of a wilderness. Still, brambles caught at Val's feet and clumps of moss almost made her slip and fall into the brittle undergrowth. She was glad she'd chosen her more sensible shoes.

Near a willow tree whose roots bulged in the soil like veins, a low rockery was covered with moss and lichen. Helen started tugging at the rocks, pulling them free and dropping them by her feet. "Help me," she said. "Some things you can't do on your own." Val joined in, throwing the flinty chunks of stone to one side. Soon they had exposed a mound of crumbly black soil. Its closeness to the estuary gave it a brackish odour. Helen paused and wiped her face. Then, with a dreamlike slowness, she opened her backpack and took out two implements: a small coal-shovel and a rock hammer. She gave Val a tired smile and said: "If anyone asks, I'm looking for fossils in the estuary."

Val watched Helen dig in the mound for a while. She wasn't keen to help, this close to finding what she suspected was there. *Why the hammer?* she thought, and didn't like the answer that came to mind. About a foot down into the soil, Helen reached some kind of cavity. She worked along its length, opening up a trench several feet long and a foot deep. Its walls were smooth and rounded. Helen stopped and looked up at the flawless blue sky. Her face was twisted with pain. "The ground couldn't hold him," she said quietly.

They didn't stay at the hotel. Helen wanted to go straight back to London. She wouldn't talk about what they'd seen. When the train went through a tunnel, she closed her eyes and wrapped her arms tight around herself. Val felt at a loss. This had gone beyond what she could manage.

When they reached Paddington Station, Helen suggested they get a drink. Over a glass of chilled wine, she gave Val a playful smile. "I'll take up your offer to come with me on the Tube," she said. "From here it's the Bakerloo line to Oxford Circus, then the Victoria line to Seven Sisters."

"All right then." Maybe it wasn't too late to help.

As they passed through the ticket gates, down the escalator and along the pale tunnels, Helen didn't really seem to be afraid. Her expression was a kind of amused defiance, like a bad girl in a 1940s *film noir*. Val half expected her to light a cigarette. When the train blazed into the tunnel, Helen stepped onto it without a backward glance.

It had obviously been another painfully hot day in London. The half-dozen people in the carriage looked worn out, even sick. No doubt the bad smell was affecting them. Was there a dead rat under one of the seats? It must have been there for a while, because they'd tried to cover it up with some cloying perfume—violets maybe, or roses, something out of season.

No-one got out of the carriage at Edgware Road, but three men got on. They must have come from some kind of workshop, because their skin looked dusty and their clothes were smeared with tar. They were either gesticulating or using a basic sign language Val hadn't seen before—either way, they were silent.

Before the next station, the train stopped in a tunnel and the light went out. "Fuck," Val said. Helen laughed, but not in amusement. A moth flew past, its wingtip brushing Val's cheek. The odour of decay was getting worse. Just as Val was about to scream, the train began to rumble forward in the dark.

When its doors opened, they were not at Victoria. It seemed to be outdoors, though Val couldn't see the sky. How had the night come on so fast? The ground beneath her feet was more like bare rock than concrete. The wind blowing from the tunnel carried a faint smell of rotting fruit. From a long way away, Val could hear voices. Whether they were chanting or crying, she wasn't sure. She reached out to Helen, and their hands clasped as they walked away from the platform. The light was so faint it was hard to be sure you were seeing anything at all. The shapes they passed could have been people waiting, or pillars, or dead trees. Val felt a dry flake touch her face, then another. She thought they were ashes until one caught on her lips and she recognised the scent of a rose petal.

The ground beneath their feet was softer now. Val could see faint lights in the distance. There was a moisture in the air, a scent of rank soil. Then the unmistakeable whisper of running water. Had they come to the Thames? Val thought she could see many people kneeling on the bank, reaching down to the current. Beside her, Helen was breathing hard. "Where is he?" she said.

Val knelt beside her and immersed her hands in the dark water. It felt colder than any unfrozen water should be, but as immaterial as mist. She tried to splash it onto her face, but her hands came up dry. And when she looked around, she realised she was alone. She got up and walked along the bank, but no-one else was there. Nor was there any bridge. But surely, if she walked far enough, the river would come to an end.

Some of Them Fell

This happened twenty-six years ago. Why I'm talking about it now isn't clear even to me, but there's a time when you have to offload certain things. A psychiatrist once told me that even when I'm telling the truth it sounds like a story. So make allowances for that. I've paid for it.

We'd come to the end of the fifth year at our north Birmingham school. What used to be called the O-level exams. Some of us stayed on and some went out into the bright world of work, parenthood, and so forth. It was the first year of a new Tory government, and those of us who imagined ourselves politically aware were saying that made no difference. Five years later, we'd see how wrong we were. But then, *absolutely nothing* you say or do at sixteen makes sense a few years later.

To celebrate our transition to the adult world, four of us were going out to the hills near Rednal on Friday night to drink wine and get stoned. There was me, my mate Dean and his girlfriend Zoe, and a boy called Adrian I hardly knew. By virtue of the usual fictions, we all had permission not to go home that night.

Zoe had got the hash from her big sister Kathy, who was something of a legend at our school after being suspended for turning up with a slashed blazer and punk haircut. She'd dropped out not long after. Zoe said hash was "small time" by Kathy's standards. Dean and I had bought the wine from a sixth-former: four bottles of red for which, in retrospect, we were robbed blind—though Adrian had paid his share without complaint.

Adrian was the kind of kid who gets bullied automatically in school: thin, pale, and short-sighted. But when provoked, he reacted with enough violence to deter all but the hardest cases. By the fifth form, he'd graduated to merely being ignored. My strongest memory of him before that night was the cross-country runs, when his lack of weight gave him an advantage over the rugby heroes. He'd streak off ahead of the pack like a white shadow, running with desperate tenacity, ending up shaky and breathless in the pavilion.

Dean was a good-looking but moody lad of mixed race who was leaving school to work in sales. Zoe was short and glamorous, a definite catch, and the only one of our group staying on for A-levels. She had something of her sister's punk tendencies, and had just celebrated her exam results with a nose piercing.

I'm not sure why Adrian was invited, except that Zoe was quite intrigued by the occult theories he used to come out with in RE lessons: clairvoyance, astral projection, all the Castaneda shit you could find in second-hand bookshops. Perhaps she thought he could add something mystical to the night's activities. If so, it was surprising that Dean wasn't suspicious of her interest in him. But in some ways Dean was the most adult of us—which is to say, he was immature as opposed to very immature.

The four of us met in the city centre around seven. It was already colder than when we'd made the plan, and I wished I'd brought a coat. Dean and Zoe were kissing in the bus shelter. Adrian was his usual withdrawn self; I couldn't work out if his half-smile was due to tension or a silent mockery of the world. Dean offered round a pack of cigarettes, and Zoe and Adrian both took one. I didn't want to commit the social gaffe of choking in public. Let alone risk dropping the two bottles of wine I was carrying in a plastic bag.

The bus crept through heavy traffic past the Northfield shopping centre and the car factory at Longbridge. It was packed with weary office and shop workers from the city centre. This would be my first summer without a long holiday: just the weekend before I signed on and started looking for jobs in the *Evening Mail*.

We got off at Rednal, spent half an hour in the amusement arcade, bought some crisps and chocolate to eat later. Then we walked on beyond the shops, until we reached a pathway up the overgrown hillside. Young and fit as we were, it was a pretty steep climb. The ground was slippery with dead leaves, but tree roots and stones gave us a purchase on the slope. The bottles that Dean and I were carrying clanked alarmingly. After ten minutes or so, we reached the long twisted spine of the hill and could see down on both sides.

In the reddish afternoon light, the wooded slopes had more than a hint of autumn even though it was midsummer. It was partly the dead trees that storms had blown over, reaching with stark limbs through the undergrowth. And partly the carpet of dead leaves that winter hadn't worn through. The light shivered through dense curtains of green and gold, but underneath there was a smell of decay. Tiny black rabbit turds were scattered across the path.

Dean and Zoe walked hand in hand, with me and Adrian following. The two of us made eye contact a few times, but didn't speak. I heard Zoe say: "This place makes me feel really strange. It's like the sea. It's not old or new, just different." I knew what she meant. Despite the occasional holiday in Wales, I was so used to the city that an absence of walls disturbed me. I was too aware of the sky, how dark it would be without streetlamps or windows.

We walked on past a stagnant pool, its surface coated with dark green algae, and came to a lookout point with a small brick tower. From here, we could see clear across the reservoir and the factories to the roofs and tower blocks of the city. Dusk was settling in the distant streets. A kestrel hovered over the slope, dropped and climbed again, negotiating an invisible landscape of air currents.

At Dean's suggestion, we left the path and wandered down the slope in search of cover. There weren't many people around, but we didn't want any witnesses to our ritual. Among the scattered trees, the ground was uneven; the soil had a gritty texture, like ash. Occasionally a bird or a rabbit moved just beyond sight. The sense of being in another world intensified: I felt suddenly very awake, ready to learn whatever secrets this place held.

When we came to the dead tree, we all seemed to realise it was the right place for us to stop. It was a cedar, I think, though it no longer had leaves. Its long, twisted branches were almost stripped of bark, and the wood underneath was black. The trunk had been split open, perhaps by lightning. Dean reached up to a branch and pulled himself onto it, his legs kicking in the air. "Be careful," Zoe said. The dead wood took his weight. He stared down at us for a few seconds before dropping back to the ground.

The light was fading now. Adrian opened his backpack and took out some red candles. "I couldn't get black ones," he said with no hint of irony, placing five candles to make a rough circle in the soil and lighting them with his thin plastic cigarette lighter. The four of us sat around the candles. Dean opened the first bottle of wine and poured some into a plastic tumbler for each of us. We raised our drinks in a silent gesture.

"The voice of the trees," said Adrian suddenly. "The memory of the rocks. The spirit of the hills." He dipped a finger into his cup of wine and touched it to his forehead, then dipped it again and flicked a red drop into the space between the candles. Then he drank. We all followed suit. I can't say it deepened the sense of mystery—if anything, it struck a note of teenage pretension where something adult had seemed within reach.

We passed the wine bottle round, refilling our cups. I felt dazed and slightly nauseous. Zoe took out some Rizlas and began, very carefully, to roll a joint. She crumbled the dark hash into the tobacco and wrapped the blend in two thicknesses of paper, not wasting a molecule. Then she lit the end, took a quick drag and passed it to Dean. When my turn came I tried not to cough, but the first mouthful burned my throat. Adrian nearly choked, for which I was grateful.

As the joint went round again, Zoe gripped Dean's hand and dug her nails into the skin. "I want to have your child," she said. I felt myself blushing, more shocked by my reaction than by her words. Her eyes were shining in the candlelight. There was a blood spot under the new gold stud on the left side of her nose.

Dean nodded calmly. "It could be arranged." He kissed her mouth. Around us, the daylight had nearly faded. I was relieved to see a half-moon shining through the dead twigs of the cedar tree. At least, if the candles went out, we wouldn't be in total darkness. To my left, I could hear Adrian saying something about how rituals could intensify the mind "like a magnesium flare". I bit my lip as waves of dark energy broke through the ring of candlelight.

We were on the second bottle of wine, and still passing the charred joint around, when a large silver-grey moth began circling over the candles. A second moth joined it, then a third. We stared at them in silence. They were like distant lights on the point of going out. I thought I could hear the flapping of their wings. The three of them seemed to be trying to make a shape in the air, but failing.

Then, suddenly, one of the moths flew into Adrian's face. He cried out and snatched at it, then trembled violently as if he'd touched an electric wire. Before any of us had reacted, the spasm passed. He was staring into the trees, his mouth slack, a thread of saliva on his chin. The moths had disappeared. Slowly, Adrian opened his right hand and reached forward into the candlelight. To me, the crushed shape looked like a tiny human foetus—but that was just the hash.

We carried on drinking, and Zoe lit another joint. "This night will go on forever," she said. The half-moon was overhead now, faintly tinged with pink. I don't remember exactly what we talked about then, but it had to do with sex—erotic dreams maybe, or slow dancing. The mood was a stoned calm with hysteria just below the surface. Adrian said something about how disciples of magic made love on the astral plane, how they said "sky-clad" instead of "naked".

I must have dozed off for a while. When I opened my eyes, the candles had blown out. Adrian was sitting hunched a few yards away, rubbing his hands—whether for warmth or to remove the last traces of the moth, I wasn't sure. At first I couldn't see where Dean and Zoe had got to. Then I saw them on the dead tree, maybe ten feet up in the air. They'd climbed into the split trunk and were wedged in there together. I watched, dry-mouthed, as they slowly removed each other's clothes and dropped them to the ground.

This wasn't bragging or wishful thinking, this was reality. I felt bad about watching them, but somehow I couldn't look away. Their bodies locked together, pulsing steadily like the walls of a heart: dark skin against pale. One of them cried out. Then I felt a hand touch my arm. I froze, but didn't pull away.

Adrian's hand moved down to my thigh, then stroked my crotch. I slipped my hand onto his. When his fingers reached for the zipper, I stopped them. "Let's go somewhere," I said. I didn't want Dean or Zoe to see us, though at that point they'd hardly have noticed a Roman orgy taking place around the dead tree.

We stood up and looked at each other. Then Adrian turned and walked down the slope; I followed close behind. We reached a line of thin trees with ferns between them, pushed through and stopped on the far side. I reached for Adrian, pulling at his arms; we kissed awkwardly. Then I noticed a weird smell coming from the bracken. A blend of decay and something else: a chemical. Adrian's hands were unfastening my belt. "Wait," I said. "There's something here."

"Some rubbish," Adrian said. "Think it's just behind you." He looked past my shoulder, then backed away. "Oh, no." I turned around, and for a moment could only see a clump of undergrowth. The smell was stronger there, and I recognised it: glue. A brown paper bag among the ferns. A pale hand gripping it.

Adrian took a small torch out of his jacket pocket. By its light, we saw two small bodies on the ground. They were boys, aged about nine or ten. It looked as though they'd come up here with glue-bags, passed out and not woken up. Then I saw a black trainer further down the slope, with a foot in it. A third boy had tried to get away, but not made it back to the road. The bodies were stiff, their faces bruised by death, their eyes dull. Something had eaten the third boy's hand.

Suddenly I couldn't breathe. The moonlight went out; I fell to my knees and vomited sour wine over the ferns. Then I wiped my mouth and stood up. Tears blurred my vision. Adrian was just standing there, frozen. "Jesus Christ," he said. "We've got to call the police."

When we got back to the dead tree, Dean and Zoe were getting dressed. I tried to explain what we'd seen. Dean wanted to go and look, but Zoe wouldn't. So Adrian led Dean to the bodies while I waited with Zoe. "Why were you down there?" she asked me. I didn't answer. For the first time since nightfall, I looked at my watch. It was nearly two o'clock.

Within a few minutes, the other two returned. Dean went straight to Zoe and hugged her, then said "We'd better go back to Rednal." Adrian was shaking from delayed shock. I touched his arm, but he flinched away. The moon was clouding over, and we were in danger of being left in complete darkness. Treading carefully on the rough slope, we climbed back to the path and walked along the crest of the hill until we could see a clear way to the road below.

In the high street, nowhere was open; the only lit windows were in the hotel. We found a call-box, and Dean phoned the police to tell them what we'd seen. He didn't give his name, just said he and his girlfriend had been on the hillside when they weren't supposed to be together. When he hung up, we walked on quickly towards Longbridge. At least the streetlights were bright.

I still felt both stoned and drunk, a combination I've avoided since. The increasingly built-up landscape was reassuring. At least, it was until Adrian muttered to me: "I feel like the city sent us a message, to remind us that we can't escape." Dean and Zoe were walking ahead of us, holding hands. I glanced at Adrian's face. His lips were grey, though the night air wasn't cold.

"They must have been there for days," I said. "It's horrible. One of them tried to go for help. They can't have had any idea the danger they were in."

Adrian shrugged. "Perhaps they chose that. You're never too young to learn the world is shit."

Neither of us mentioned what had almost happened between us. Speaking for myself, that wasn't down to embarrassment or second thoughts. It was the dead faces. We'd gone in search of revelation, and got far more than we were ready for. It would be a while before I was able to think about desire.

By the time we got to Longbridge, the grey steel arc joining the two sides of the factory, the lack of sleep was beginning to tell on all of us. There was a cab firm on the main road; we pooled our cash and split it three ways, an act of sharing that was already out of keeping with the times. Dean intended to sneak Zoe into his house; Adrian and I were getting separate cabs home. Our prepared versions of tonight were forgotten. From now on, reality would have to fend for itself.

About six months later, I ran into Dean in the Palisades shopping centre. He was wearing a pinstriped suit, and his hair was cropped very short. We talked for a few minutes. He'd split up with Zoe, and was seeing an "older woman"—with the lofty maturity of nineteen—who had her own car. He was learning to drive.

"Are you still in touch with Adrian?" he asked. I shook my head. His face clouded. "That was a bad business. Especially for him—you know he lost his sister a few years ago."

"I didn't know that," I said. Remembering how cut off I'd been from whatever the other kids were talking about in school.

"Didn't he tell you? I thought you two were pretty close."

"Not that close," I said.

Dean glanced at me, as if not sure what I meant. "Good to see you, Matt," he said. "Take care."

It was another year before I saw Adrian again. By then, I was eighteen and had discovered night life. I had a job behind the cash till at a dry cleaner's and a tiny studio flat in Balsall Heath. Belatedly, I was learning to talk to people—if only as a means to the end of not being alone.

A few times, I went to the Jug off Livery Street. The entrance was all but hidden, an unmarked door under a railway bridge. The owner was a middle-aged man in an expensive lounge suit and make-up. The interior was a kitsch museum: Garbo film posters, velvet-covered sofas, Tiffany lamps. The wall of one room was a rockery with water trickling down it, electric lights glowing red and green and purple through the murmuring stream.

One January night, I spotted a nervous-looking young man standing on his own near the cabaret stage in the main bar. Later there might be a torch singer or a bad comedian, but for now the stage was empty. I'd already decided to talk to him before I realised it was Adrian.

He seemed glad to see me—partly, I think, because any familiar face was welcome in a place like that. I also realised that his apparently nervous state was not so much psychological as physical: his hands trembled slightly, and there was a faint tic in the corner of his mouth. But he said he was well. He was working in a bank now, a job not unlike mine in its financial basis and mind-numbing tedium.

I bought him a vodka and orange. We had the usual conversation about where we hung out. The one thing we didn't mention was the past. Like me, he was far from impressed with the Jug. "Half the guys in here look like they haven't had sex since 1959," he said. "And it's now 23:17." That made me laugh.

We had a couple more drinks, and endured the worst Shirley Bassey imitation I've ever seen (and I've seen a few). The night began to take on the unreal glow of alcohol and desire. Adrian gripped my hand and kissed the knuckles. I wondered if it was just unfinished business, but still invited him back to my flat. "That'd be nice," he said. "You don't want to see my place, it's a ruin. They filmed *Tombs of the Blind Dead* there. And I live in Wolverhampton, it's a long journey on the night bus."

Outside, the streets were papered over with frost. We walked together up Livery Street, over the frozen canal, and on to the taxi rank in Colmore Row. Adrian seemed withdrawn as we waited in the queue; I assumed he was drunk, or nervous of the people around us. Finally our turn came, and we sat shivering on the cab's plastic back seat.

The taxi drove up Barford Street, a mile of grey office blocks and red-brick industrial buildings. We were just on the edge of Balsall Heath when I noticed how badly Adrian's hands were shaking. "Are you cold?" I asked. He stared at me in panic. His face was covered with sweat. His hands were moving rapidly from side to side in front of him, flickering in the half-light as if working the shutters on a loom. Suddenly he clapped a hand over his mouth. I shouted to the driver: "Please stop the car. My friend's sick." He pulled up to the kerb, and I reached past Adrian to open the door on his side. He fell out onto the frost-smeared pavement and lay there on his side, half curled up.

I jumped out. He was twitching, banging his head against the paving-stone. I pressed my hand against the lower side of his face and tried to hold him still. It was like there was a cry buried deep inside him that couldn't get out. He vomited suddenly, and I pulled him away from it. The Asian taxi driver was standing beside me, silent. "I don't know what's wrong," I said. "He wasn't even drunk."

"It's a fit. He needs an ambulance. I can't take him to hospital, I'm not qualified to look after him. Stay here and I'll call an ambulance for you."

By the time the ambulance came, its light flashing but no siren, Adrian had quietened down. But he was still unconscious and shuddering; his hair was stuck to his pale forehead. I paid the taxi driver, who didn't charge much. Two paramedics took Adrian into the ambulance, where they trussed him like a hostage.

I spent two hours in casualty, watching Adrian writhe in the grip of an unreal sleep. His eyes were open, but he didn't see anything. Eventually, he lay still and the muscles of his face relaxed. Then he raised his head, saw me sitting by the bed and said: "Get me out of here."

"Wait till the morning," I said. "You've been out for a long time. You passed out in the taxi. How are you feeling?"

"Shit." He reached for my hand; I felt the tremor in his fingers. "Thanks for waiting."

"No problem. Are you going to be okay?" He didn't respond. I wrote my phone number on a scrap of paper and passed it to him. "Call me soon, Adrian. Let me know how you are."

The charge nurse asked me for my number as well. I phoned for a taxi from casualty, then waited outside. The sky was cloudy: no moon or stars, only the streetlamps and the trapped light of the city.

The hospital called me late the next morning and asked me to take Adrian home. So I got to see his flat in Wolverhampton, which was chaotic but not much worse than mine. The blank walls were less claustrophobic than the trapped look in his eyes. "I have to get away," he said. "But where?"

We met up the next weekend, and soon got into a low-key relationship. We had to be careful, of course: the law was different then. But also, I found him withdrawn most of the time—sometimes annoyingly so. When he did try to be affectionate, I sensed a terrible loneliness inside him that I couldn't reach; and if I did, I suspected it would freeze me. The sardonic wit he'd developed since leaving school was a defence mechanism: underneath, he was deeply afraid.

I never saw him undergo a *grand mal* seizure again, but a couple of times he told me he'd recently had one. At home, where no-one could help him. I was worried about that, but he said there was nothing anyone could do. "If I have an accident, that's how it goes." That sounded like an echo of the karmic crap he'd espoused at school, though he said he'd forgotten that stuff. When recovering from a fit he was worse than usual: pale and shaky, a watercolour of himself.

Two things stay in my mind from the first night we spent together (apart from certain things that are none of your business). The first is that the way he slept was like the way I'd seen him lying on the pavement: on his side, with his knees half drawn up. Later, in a union first-aid course, I learned that was called "the recovery position"— the position you should put someone in if they passed out.

The second thing happened shortly before dawn. We were in my flat. I woke up with a vague impression of passing lights, probably due to cars on the road outside. Adrian was asleep, but I could see his shoulders twitching in the grainy half-light of the streetlamp outside the window. I leaned over him. His hands were making the same weaving movements I'd seen in the taxi. Something pale and almost, but not quite, luminous was passing back and forth between them. It had wings, but they were crushed.

The room suddenly felt very cold. I wondered if I should wake Adrian. Would that make it worse? I didn't know exactly what I was afraid of. It seemed better to do nothing. I slipped back to my own side of the bed, facing him. Eventually he went back into normal sleep, where I tried (without success) to join him.

I did succeed in getting him to throw out a lot of the rubbish that cluttered up his flat, so he was less at risk of injuring himself or starting a fire. I also persuaded him not to drink so much when we were together. He'd been in the habit of getting drunk when he went out on his own, to give himself confidence. The fact that I was able to make him take better care of himself reassured me that he wasn't as self-destructive as his attitude suggested.

However, we did get drunk together once. We'd decided to go out for dinner and then had a pointless argument about politics. Adrian supported the Falklands War, I didn't. By the time we got to the restaurant, our mood had deteriorated and I considered going home alone. But we ordered a meal and then had to wait a long time for it. Making inroads into the bottle of wine seemed the only option. The more Adrian went on about the realities of the modern world—how any attempt at a planned or equal society was doomed to failure by the intrinsic selfishness of human nature—the more immature he seemed. Eventually my temper snapped.

"So where exactly does your profound knowledge of human nature come from?" I said. "You keep saying you're disillusioned, but you've just swapped one mystical guru for another. You're in love with images of power. You want a reason to believe most people are inferior, so you can feel less worthless. Just be honest for once. You're weak and scared and you know nothing."

That got to him. He went quiet and started drinking faster. I didn't bother to stop him. In hindsight, of course, I was guilty of similar things—with insensitivity on top of them. Whoever said *"In vino veritas"* assumed there was only one truth to tell, but we're all full of competing voices and conflicting views. At least the argument ended there. Adrian started reminiscing about the occult books he'd read back in the seventies: spirit photographs and astral bodies and ectoplasm. We ordered a second bottle of wine.

Back at my flat, Adrian was sick in the bathroom. I was afraid he'd go into a seizure—and it would be partly my fault—but he just lay on the couch, staring into the gas fire. His hands slowly moved up in front of his face; he gazed between them, as if trying to remember the weaving movements I'd seen before. "They were looking for me," he said.

"Who were?" I knelt beside the couch and put my arms around Adrian. His eyes seemed much older than the rest of his face. "Not the children?"

"Not them exactly. I don't fucking know." He shivered; the tremor went through me. "Do you ever feel like your life has already happened?"

"Only when I'm with you. Why?"

"My sister Clare—did you know I had a sister? She was two years older than me, went to the grammar school. When I was eleven, she started having problems there. Other girls picking on her. Telling her she was ugly, she'd never get a man, that kind of thing. They used to put sketches of her, and worse things, in her desk. One time she came home crying. Told me she didn't know what to do.

"What did I know? I was twelve. I told her not to go to the teachers or tell our parents, because then she'd be a snitch. She should stand up to them. I think she tried for another month. Then she put ground glass in her dinner and ate it in the school canteen. Nobody saw.

"She came home and went straight to bed. I went into her room to ask if she was okay. She didn't say anything.

Her breathing sounded . . . torn. Mum phoned an ambulance, but it was too late. Clare died in hospital around midnight. She left her diary on the bed. The last entry was that day. It just said, *'No way out.'*"

He turned away from me and curled up on the sofa. His eyes were still open, but I couldn't get any response from him. I held him for a while until he fell asleep. Then I carried him, with some effort, to the bed and pulled the duvet over him. I lay awake in the dark for a while, hearing the cars drive past, and now and then a siren wailing a long way off. It occurred to me that real sirens were the opposite of the myth: instead of calling people, they had to find them.

In March, as the weather brightened, Adrian's mood seemed to improve. We went for a walk along the Grand Union Canal, past derelict factories and walls topped with razor-wire; and around Edgbaston Reservoir, where the wind made silvery cuts in the grey water. He was working up to it, of course. But I was still surprised when he asked me to go to Rednal with him, to the hills. Neither of us had been back there since the summer of 1980.

It was late afternoon when we got off the bus outside the arcade. The sunlight was glinting from windows and steel fences. We found the path we'd used before. The hillside was slick with mud and rotting leaves. Most of the trees were black silhouettes. We climbed to the crest of the hill, walked on past the stagnant pool and the lookout point, then turned down the slope. I couldn't have said where the dead tree was, but I knew we'd get there.

The five red candles were still in the ground, though the pentagram Adrian had marked between them had faded. He relit the candles with a plastic lighter, and we sat down on opposite sides of the circle. The wavering flames gave me a sudden feeling of time being unreal: not just the past two years, but all my life. Adrian took a half-bottle of whisky out of his bag. "I'm not sure about this," I said.

He looked at me calmly. "I have to." He poured most of the whisky into two glasses and we drank it slowly, feeling its addictive heat soak into us. The daylight was beginning to fade, the sun setting on the far side of the hill. *This night will go on forever.* Mercifully, we hadn't brought anything to smoke.

A faint after-image of moon glowed above the trees. We didn't say much. This wasn't a new beginning for us. Indeed, I didn't fool myself that it was about Adrian and me at all. He tipped his head back, drained his whisky in a long shuddering gulp. Then he leaned forward and stared into the dark space between the candles. In front of him, his hands began to move slowly: together, apart, back together, working the shuttles of an invisible loom.

Threads of light began to appear between his hands, crossing each other, forming a whitish cat's cradle. He crouched over, staring into the web, his limbs starting to tremble. I was afraid he'd go into a fit. Then, suddenly, his mouth opened and I heard him choking for breath. His throat swelled. I got up, ready to help him breathe. Before I could reach him, a silver-grey misshapen thing struggled out of his mouth and dropped to the ground. It was like a moth, and also like a foetus, but horribly crippled and slow. The web of light didn't catch it.

I watched, helpless, as another grey creature escaped from his throat, flapped its shattered wings, and lay still on the grass. Adrian's face was distorted with pain. His hands were still weaving back and forth, restoring the broken threads of light. His mouth stretched to let a third shape crawl free. Then the tension left him, and he slumped onto the ground.

I knelt over him, close to panic. But he hadn't gone into a seizure. I found the whisky and poured some into his mouth. The sky was dark by now, the moon and stars clouded over. The candles were still burning. Where the moths had fallen, a few grey flakes of ash stirred in the grass. *Three for the price of one*, I thought, and almost laughed. A cold breeze made the candles flicker.

A few minutes later, Adrian shivered and opened his eyes. "Are you okay? " I said. He didn't answer. "We'd better go." I took his hand and led him back to the crest of the hill, then down to the road. He seemed to be in a trance.

As we waited for the bus, he glanced back to where the moonlight picked out a few gaunt trees on the hillside. "It's gone," he said. There was a look on his face I recognised from older people I knew. The loss and guilt were still there, but they were under the surface. We were both very tired.

By the time we got back to Birmingham, it was late. We both had work in the morning. I suggested getting some food, but Adrian wanted to go home. I waited with him near Snow Hill, at the top of the expressway. The traffic noise was drowned by the silence in my head. "I'll call you," he said. I knew our affair was over, but it didn't matter. For him, it had only been a means to an end. Maybe that's true of most people, if you accept that the end is more than the obvious things.

When the bus came, he touched my cheek and said, "Thanks. I couldn't have done that on my own." Surprised, and briefly upset, I watched the lights of the bus diminish as it sped downhill and on through the night. If I could, maybe the city would let him go.

Acknowledgements

The publisher would like to thank Ella Lane,
Mat Joiner, Meggan Kehrli, Ken Mackenzie,
Mark Morris, Polly Rose Morris, Jim Rockhill,
Nicholas Royle, and Nel Whatmore.

"Sight Unseen"
was first published in *Lovecraft Unbound*,
edited by Ellen Datlow,
Dark Horse Books, 2009.

"Crow's Nest"
was first published in *Shadows & Tall Trees*,
Autumn 2010, edited by Michael Kelly,
Undertow Books, 2010.

"All the Shadows"
was first published in *Wilde Stories*,
edited by Steve Berman, Lethe Press, 2011.

"Midnight Flight"
was first published in
The Horror Anthology of Horror Anthologies,
edited by D.F. Lewis, Megazanthus Press, 2011.

About the Author

Joel Lane (1963-2013) was born in Exeter, but lived most of his life in Birmingham, where many of his stories are set. In addition to two novels, *From Blue to Black* (2000) and *The Blue Mask* (2003), Lane was the author of numerous collections, including the British Fantasy Award-winning *The Earth Wire* (1994), *The Lost District* (2006), and *The Terrible Changes* (2009). *Where Furnaces Burn* won the World Fantasy Award for best collection in 2013.

Swan River Press

Founded in 2003, Swan River Press is an independent publishing company, based in Dublin, Ireland, dedicated to gothic, supernatural, and fantastic literature. We specialise in limited edition hardbacks, publishing fiction from around the world with an emphasis on Ireland's contributions to the genre.

www.swanriverpress.ie

*"Handsome, beautifully made volumes . . .
altogether irresistible."*

– Michael Dirda, *Washington Post*

*"It [is] often down to small, independent, specialist presses
to keep the candle of horror fiction flickering . . . "*

– Darryl Jones, *Irish Times*

*"Swan River Press has emerged as one of the most inspiring
new presses over the past decade. Not only are the books
beautifully presented and professionally produced, but they
aspire consistently to high literary quality and originality,
ranging from current writers of supernatural/weird fiction
to rare or forgotten works by departed authors."*

– Peter Bell, *Ghosts & Scholars*

THE DUMMY
& Other Uncanny Stories

Nicholas Royle

Nicholas Royle's stories are "immaculately sinister", according to Olivia Laing in the *Times Literary Supplement*, while Phil Baker, in the *Sunday Times*, described Royle as "a real craftsman of disquiet".

In his third collection, *The Dummy & Other Uncanny Stories*, Royle focuses on archetypes and phenomena that, through their particular melding of the familiar and the unfamiliar, produce uneasy, or uncanny, effects. In these stories he writes about doppelgängers, ghosts, dummies, disconnected body parts, impaired vision, the dead and the prospect of death, not without a macabre sense of humour.

These stories reflect Royle's continuing development as an exponent of the form, in which he is always seeking to learn and to grow, and to push against boundaries.

"Royle's dark fiction is always worth reading . . .
His storytelling is impeccable, his plots always interesting
and his characters credible."

– Mario Guslandi, *SFRevu*

WRITTEN BY DAYLIGHT

John Howard

Sunsets in a London suburb, and a transformation into an Earthly paradise; paths winding through a Transylvanian palace gardens, and an obsessed journey towards a Mediterranean dream; a city so ancient that even its total disappearance has been forgotten, and an island of shifting sands that can never be truly mapped . . . The vivid and diverse settings of these stories are façades obscuring reality for the exiles and outcasts who find their way into them. Seemingly born out of time and place, they seek the right routes to bring them to where they want to be, but there are many diversions on the way. In these stories of haunted landscapes and intimidating cities many possibilities confront the unwary, but there is usually only one choice to be made.

"Howard's work is both delicate and powerful."

– The Agony Column

"If there is a unifying theme here it is the transience
of existence, from the individual to the social
and even the geographical . . . not only well-written
but also offer remarkable ideas."

– Supernatural Tales

"Most of these tales are so subtle as to defy
any category of the strange at all, but reward
re-reading and are all the greater for it."

– The Pan Review

YOU'LL KNOW WHEN YOU GET THERE

Lynda E. Rucker

A woman returns home to revisit an encounter with the numinous; couples take up residence in houses full of sinister secrets; a man fleeing a failed marriage discovers something ancient and unknowable in rural Ireland . . .

In her introduction, Lisa Tuttle observes that "certain places are doomed, dangerous in some inexplicable, metaphysical way", and the characters in these stories all seem drawn in their own ways to just such places, whether trying to return home or endeavouring to get as far from life as possible. These nine stories by Shirley Jackson Award winner Lynda E. Rucker tell tales of those lost and searching, often for something they cannot name, and encountering along the way the uncanny embedded in the everyday world.

"Indirection is a special skill and it's one that Lynda E. Rucker uses frequently to emphasise those near indefinable moments of social alienation and paranoia, that you just want to get up and run far, far away from."

– Adam L. G. Nevill

"Lynda is the genuine article—a serious, literary author of 'quiet horror' whose work is disquieting, inspiring, and oddly reassuring. It's good to know that there are writers so gifted working in our genre."

– Supernatural Tales